WITHDRAWN

ALSO BY DAVID YOUNG

POETRY

Black Lab
At the White Window
Night Thoughts and Henry Vaughan
The Planet on the Desk: Selected and New Poems

NONFICTION

Seasoning: A Poet's Year

TRANSLATIONS

The Poetry of Petrarch
Out on the Autumn River: Selected Poems of Du Mu
The Clouds Float North: The Complete Poems of Yu Xuanji
The Book of Fresh Beginnings: Selected Poems of Rainer Maria Rilke
Intensive Care: Selected Poems of Miroslav Holub
Five T'ang Poets
The Duino Elegies: A New Translation

CRITICISM

Six Modernist Moments in Poetry
The Action to the Word: Style and Structure in Shakespearean Tragedy
Troubled Mirror: A Study of Yeats's "The Tower"
The Heart's Forest: Shakespeare's Pastoral Plays
Something of Great Constancy: The Art of "A Midsummer Night's Dream"

Du Fu

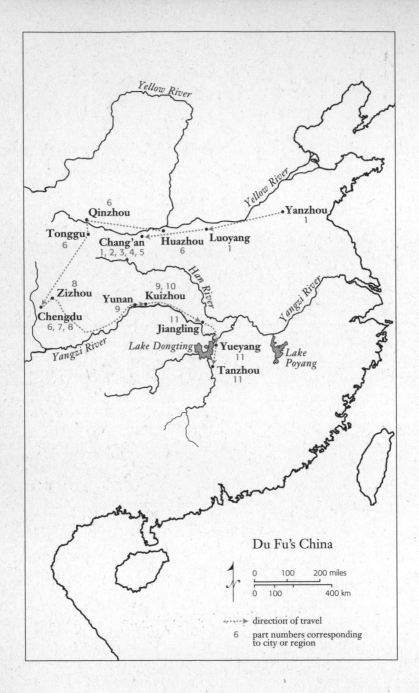

Yellow River

Yellow River

6
Qinzhou

Tonggu
6

Chang'an
1, 2, 3, 4, 5

Huazhou
6

Luoyang
1

Yanzhou
1

Han River

8
Zizhou

Yunan
9

9, 10
Kuizhou

Chengdu
6, 7, 8

Yangzi River

Jiangling
11

Yangzi River

Lake Dongting

Yueyang
11

Lake
Poyang

Tanzhou
11

Du Fu's China

0   100   200 miles

0   100   400 km

N

direction of travel

6   part numbers corresponding
to city or region

Du Fu

A LIFE IN POETRY

Translated by David Young

ALFRED A. KNOPF
New York 2008

THIS IS A BORZOI BOOK
PUBLISHED BY ALFRED A. KNOPF

www.aaknopf.com

Knopf, Borzoi Books, and the colophon are registered
trademarks of Random House, Inc.

Grateful acknowledgment is made to Harvard University Press for
permission to reprint excerpts from *Tu Fu: China's Greatest Poet* by William
Hung, copyright © 1952 by the President and Fellows of Harvard College
(Cambridge, Mass.: Harvard University Press, pp. 5, 35–38, 114, 183,
261–263, 325, 339). Reprinted by permission of Harvard University Press.

Library of Congress Cataloging-in-Publication Data

Du, Fu, 712–770.
[Poems. English. Selections]
Du Fu : a life in poetry / poems by Du Fu ; translated by David Young.
p. cm.
Includes bibliographical references.
ISBN 978-0-375-71160-2
1. Du, Fu, 712–770—Translations into English.   I. Young, David.
II. Title.
PL2675.A285 2008
895.1'13—dc22
2008016773

Manufactured in the United States of America
First Edition

Contents

2. Back at the Capital, 745–750

3. War and Rebellion, 750–755

4. Trapped in the Capital, 756–758

5. Reunion and Recovery, 758–759

6. On the Move, 759

9. East to Kuizhou, 765–766

10. The Gentleman Farmer, 767–768

11. Last Days

Introduction

The Tang dynasty (618–907 AD) was perhaps the greatest age for poetry that the history of civilization has known. This means, of course, that it produced many outstanding poets. Yet one in particular, Du Fu (712–770), is singled out even among his great contemporaries. Why is he seen as the most accomplished of them all?

That question is trickier to answer than one might think. An English reader, encountering Du Fu in an anthology of poetry, or even in a volume of his selected poems, may find him admirable without necessarily wanting to put him above such masterful contemporaries and slightly later poets as Wang Wei, Li Bai, Hanshan, Li He, or Bo Juyi. Yet generations of Chinese readers have been firm and unwavering in considering him their greatest poet. Their reverence is unmistakable, and it deserves our notice. This book is my attempt to address the question of Du Fu's greatness.

Primary to that effort, of course, are fresh translations of the poems, in versions as clear and expressive as I know how to make them. There are already many exceptional translations of Du Fu in English, and they range all the way from prose versions that attempt to be as literal as possible to versions that try, in one way or another, to adhere to the formal properties and characteristic conventions of the poem in Chinese. Over the years I have evolved a kind of middle way, whereby the Chinese line (which is also a complete syntactic unit, comparable to the sentence) is treated as a free verse stanza, usually a couplet, with a minimum of punctuation. This method allows me to reflect some of the formal properties of the originals (e.g., their extensive use of parallelism) without feeling restricted by conventions that are comfortable in one language but often strained or awkward in another.

I have been reading and translating Du Fu for many years now, and some of my translations have been through numerous versions. I have relied, variously, on my limited knowledge of Chinese, on Chinese-English dictionaries, on other versions in English, on scholarly and critical discussions, on the help and advice of friends, and most of all, perhaps, on my growing sense of how Chinese poetics and Tang dynasty conventions shaped and were shaped by the poets.

My being able to situate a poet like Du Fu in the poetic practices of his time is more important, finally, than any fluency in Chinese. Knowing the literal meaning of a group of characters is merely the first step, even for native speakers and readers, toward a successful interpretation of a poetic text. The translator's job is first to interpret the poem and then to negotiate an effective version of it in the language to which the original is migrating. When the process is successful, especially when poets are involved at both ends, the translator inhabits the other poet's world and imagination, an exhilarating merging of sensibilities and a replicating of the creative process that can make translating addictive. To the extent realizable, I have tried to capture Du Fu's idiosyncratic voice and outlook in a poetic mode that will be both as comfortable and as compelling to English-speaking readers as Du Fu himself was to his contemporaries.

In addition, though, I aim to demonstrate how Du Fu developed. He began as a good poet and turned himself into a great poet, and he did this in an unprecedented fashion, widening his subject matter steadily, complicating his worldview, taking in more and more of the totality of existence, even as the social fabric around him was disrupted and devastated. As his society, one of the world's great civilizations, slipped from a golden age into chaos and uncertainty, he responded imaginatively, with poems whose excellence still startles us. His unique development is partly a matter of artistic growth, which we see of course in many poets, and partly the response of the imagination to what Wallace Stevens called "the pressure of reality." In bad times, as a kind of reaction, artists may well produce their best work. Yeats and Rilke come to mind as examples. Paul Celan, Czeslaw Milosz, and Miroslav Holub might be cited as well. A remarkable and spirited rejoinder to the disasters and contingencies of history: that is certainly one useful way to characterize the achievement of Du Fu.

Responsive to the poetic tradition that came down to him, Du Fu somehow managed to be both extremely personal and astonishingly impersonal. He wove his poems out of the materials that surrounded him: the vast existence of the natural world; the uncertain course of empire, periodically engulfed in disruptive civil wars; the misfortunes and pleasures of his own family, immediate and extended; his relations with fellow poets and scholars; the hard lives of ordinary people, so often overlooked; the changing seasons and the lives of creatures who shared his environment. He was not afraid to make an example of himself, even to the point of bitter self-mockery. Yet we never feel that he was selfish or self-centered. On the contrary, his compassion for the largely unsung peasantry of his country, and for animals, birds, and insects, is justly famous.

A paradox, then, surrounds this poet's canon: biography is irrelevant, but it is also crucial: to know his work is to know his life, with an unusual intimacy and insight. And to know the life is to appreciate fully the scope and power of the poetry. Our relation to Du Fu, if we are fortunate enough to become his readers, grows gradually into something unique and unforgettable. This is the reason, I think, for the deeply personal cherishing of both the man and the work by generation after generation of Chinese readers, over many centuries. If we Western readers read him well, we too can participate in his life's great journey and come away the wiser for it. He echoes Theodore Roethke's refrain—"I learn by going where I have to go."

The organization of this book therefore places great emphasis on the poet's life—a life we know about in detail almost solely because of the way his poems document it. From the surviving corpus of some 1,400 poems, I have chosen 170 that are firmly tied to the progress of that life; taken together they constitute a remarkable journey both in space and in time. As the poet aged, he also moved around in the China of his day, from east to west, and from north to south, usually out of necessity, and one result is that he got to know his country, its peoples and its features, with a detail and authority that few of his contemporaries could match.

I have presented the stages of this journey in eleven parts, or chapters, moving from Du Fu's early maturity to his old age and death. Each part has a very brief introduction, and many of the poems have notes, but I assume here that, properly selected and arranged, the poems mostly tell their own story, enacting Du Fu's life-journey vividly and movingly, even after thirteen centuries.

We sometimes speak rather glibly of the relation between art and life, as well as the relation between the artist and the work. Du Fu will not allow us to be glib. His response to the world around him, to the vicissitudes of history and the grandeurs of landscape, exceeds our capacity to generalize. At the same time, he is willing to incorporate homely details—chasing chickens around his yard, listening to the chirp of a cricket, receiving a gift of some shallots from a neighbor—that many poets would find too trivial to mention. The result is a significant expansion of what a poem can include, along with the idea that a poem may move through many levels of significance and feeling in a brief presentation. In that sense, we can say that Du Fu is the poet who truly originated the lyric poem as we presently know and value it. When we contemporary poets combine the profound and the trivial, drawing on our own works and days, "Du Fu," as a young poet said to me recently, "has our back."

One modest example must suffice here as illustration. The following short poem comes from a relatively tranquil period in the poet's life; he is aging and disappointed, but he loves the place where he has settled, the thatched cottage he built near Chengdu as he began the last decade of his life:

I AM A MADMAN

My thatched cottage stands
just west of Thousand Mile Bridge

this Hundred Flower Stream
would please a hermit fisherman

bamboo sways in the wind
graceful as any court beauty

rain makes the lotus flowers
even more red and fragrant

but I no longer hear from friends
who live on princely salaries

my children are always hungry
with pale and famished faces

does a madman grow more happy
before he dies in the gutter?

I laugh at myself—a madman
growing older, growing madder.

In the first half of the poem we mainly find pastoral contentment. Aware of his surroundings, attuned to the spring season, the poet has nothing but praise for his circumstances; he is glad to be alive in them. Then, perhaps provoked by his own admiration of bamboos and lotus flowers, he remembers his life in the glamorous capital and the contrast between his aborted career and the wealth and ease of his more successful friends, close to the court and enjoying royal patronage. His poverty, a constant source of worry and distress, overwhelms him yet again. Concern about feeding his family has been the story of his life for many years now. How, given that, can he experience happiness? The answer must be a sort of paradox: if a madman, dying in utter poverty, is capable of ecstasy at the end, in the gutter, then Du Fu is too. He laughs at his own mixed emotions and faces his death with an odd sense of joy. His poverty, age, illness, and approaching death ought to depress him; his joy must seem to most people a kind of madness.

The poem performs what we might describe as two emotional somersaults. But the most remarkable thing about it is the apparent effortlessness with which it does that, using the simplest details and an economy of presentation that few poets can rival.

That said, the poem must be fitted into its context, the life-journey I spoke about, to have its fullest meaning and greatest resonance. It was written at a time when Du Fu and his family were enjoying a tentative peace and happiness, a respite from their sense of exile and uncertainty. This poem takes its place in a cautious, but increasingly confident, celebration of rural life (this book's seventh part) that is truly unforgettable. Providing such context is the rationale for this book, where the art and the life are set forth in all their remarkable interdependency.

Do we have something here like *The Prelude*, the long auto-biographical poem that Wordsworth wrote about his formation as a poet? I don't think the comparison is especially useful. Wordsworth was working retrospectively, looking back at his childhood and youth, and he was self-consciously trying for a sort of epic poem on a poet's growth, an "egotistical sublime." Du Fu is much more occasional, reactive, and improvisatory. He lets certain circumstances provoke poems "of the moment." He may revise them, and he may well rearrange their circumstances for the sake of greater symmetry or beauty. But he works as he goes, seldom looking back, and he has nothing epic or integrated in mind by his practice. If, after we have surveyed the whole, we feel that a remarkable life has been expressed in remarkable poetry, that is all well and good. But Western ideas about grand artistic designs should not be imposed on a culture that was content to live in the moment, even while it revered the past, and that valued the moment for its own sake rather than for some extrinsic meaning or relation to a totalizing system. Du Fu was well acquainted with all three of the philosophic/religious traditions that were influential in his culture—Confucianism, Daoism, and Buddhism—and he made use of them all at different moments. But he was never content simply to propound their teachings. Like many of the literati, Du Fu did not adhere absolutely to any one of these philosophical traditions, but he benefited from all of them.

Through roughly three decades, his thirties, forties, and fifties, Du Fu took his art to forms of accomplishment and rich possibilities that were and are unprecedented. This book attempts to foreground the distinctive nature of that artistic achievement, its growth and fruition, as fully as possible.

I have accompanied the poems with a footnote cross-referencing the most comprehensive and useful presentation of Du Fu in English, that of William Hung. The numbers given in the footnotes are the poem numbers in his *Tu Fu: China's Greatest Poet* (Cambridge, Mass.: Harvard University Press, 1952). I describe my debt to him, and others, in the acknowledgments and bibliography, but I should like to close this introduction by reminding readers that we live in a poetic climate that has been particularly hospitable to the Chinese tradition, one begun perhaps by Ezra Pound and Arthur Waley, and more recently sponsored, in various ways, by poets who have also personally encouraged me, like Gary Snyder, Franz Wright, Charles Wright, and Charles Simic. It was the latter who wrote, when I told him who I was working on: *"Du Fu, eh? I knew him when he was Tu Fu. A swell guy!"*

A swell guy, indeed, whom readers will continue to discover and love for centuries to come.

Oberlin
October 2007

1. Early Years in the East, 737–744

In this period of his life, his twenties and early thirties, Du Fu had failed the Imperial examination at the capital, Chang'an, and had moved to Yanzhou and then to the eastern capital at Luoyang. Here he met Li Bai (Li Po), eleven years older and already a famous and innovative poet. The friendship between the two poets was undoubtedly the most significant formative element in Du Fu's artistic development. Given his disappointment in the examinations, the notion of the poet-scholar as a kind of hermit or recluse was already attractive to Du Fu, and along with Li Bai, who had been sent away from the court, he experimented with the role, in both his life and his poems. But he was too young, too ambitious, and of too limited means to make a permanent commitment to being a scholarly recluse.

A crescent moon has set
behind the windy forest

outside, an untouched lute
grows wet with dew

unseen, gurgling, the little creek
winds among the flowers

over the thatched roof
thousands of spring stars

———

We look up words in books
by the candles' shrinking light

we sip our cups and praise
our host's ancestral sword

our poems done, we chant them,
using the Wu dialect

I will remember best
the mention of Fan Li's boat.

———

(HUNG 1.) Candles were sometimes used to time a poetry contest. *Fan Li's boat:* refusing rewards for his service to the state, Fan Li (ca. fifth century BCE) climbed into a little boat and sailed away. Already the alternative life makes its appearance.

I'm in this eastern province
to pay respects to my parents

first chance I've had to see
the view from this south tower

floating clouds make a bridge
from Mount Tai to the ocean

on the huge plain, old territories
scene of ancient dynasties

a tyrant had his monument
up on that lonely peak

and a prince's ruined palace
stood in that distant city

I love the past
I always have

the others climb back down
I linger on up here.

(HUNG 2.) *Yanzhou:* a prefectural city, not far from the ocean in present-day
Shandong province. Mount Tai is to the north.

3. GAZING AT MOUNT TAI

How to describe a peak
that has produced such reverence?

there's the greenness that surrounds it—
two provinces, Qi and Lu

all creation is contained
on those dark slopes, that sunny side

layers of clouds refresh
climber and climbed alike

the birds fly up and up
beyond our straining eyes

someday I want to stand
right there on the summit

the other mountains dwarfed
spreading in all directions!

(HUNG 3.) Mount Tai is one of China's five "sacred mountains." The dark and sunny
slopes represent yin and yang, hence "all creation."

One of those famous
Mongolian horses

supple and wiry
built for speed

ears erect
like bamboo shoots

hoofs that seem
to ride the wind

you can go anywhere
on this one

trust him
with your life

you feel you're flying
and you cover

enormous distances
in just one day.

(HUNG 4.) Burton Watson notes that "Ferghana in Central Asia was renowned for
its fine horses." He dates this poem "around 741," i.e., when the poet was around
the age of twenty-nine.

Memorable portrait
of a blue falcon

the white silk
gives off wind and frost

is he watching fiercely
for a rabbit?

angry foreigner
he looks at me askance

he has a chain and ring
ready to unfasten

I could almost
take him off his perch

send him out to find
some of those little larks

scatter blood and feathers
on the prairie.

(HUNG 5.) Around 742? Hung comments about this poem and the previous one that while they "could be assigned to some other period of the poet's life" they "seem best to fit with the days of roaming on horseback and playing with hunting falcons."

6. A WINTER VISIT TO THE TEMPLE OF "HIS MYSTICAL MAJESTY" NORTH OF LUOYANG

This place is sacred to Lao Zi
a mystic capital below the pole star

fences run up the hill
to keep intruders out

the priest in charge is strict
about the ceremonies

the guards make sure
that everything is safe

———

Winter came early but the green roof tiles
keep out the cold

the golden pillar in the courtyard
transmits a cosmic unity

mountains and rivers
adorn the painted doors

sun and moon revolve
among the roof beams

———

The plum tree's spreading roots
are strong

the generations are compared
to orchids, very aptly

historians got it wrong
about Lao Zi

but now our emperor
has honored him completely

———

Many great painters
no doubt deserve their fame

but Wu Daoxuan
may be the finest

he brings the landscape
right indoors

his scenes shine
upon the temple walls

———

Five sages walk
in dragon robes

a line of scholars stretches
like a thousand wild geese

every tassel, on each headpiece,
shines and dazzles

every banner
seems to flutter

———

The temple grounds—green cedars
casting their deep shadows

touched by a hard frost
the pears turn red

jade pendants on the eaves
jingle in the wind

standing above the wellhead—
the frozen windlass

———

A dynasty fell, they say,
when he retired

and when they preserved his writings
Han emperors prospered

if I purge my spirit
of excess

might I not also
lose my clumsiness?

(HUNG 6.) Luoyang was on the Yellow River, between the two capitals. The poem contemplates the new prestige of Daoism (as opposed to Confucianism) under the Tang ruling family, hence the lines about Lao Zi (Lao Tsu), seen as its founder. The plum tree section compliments their rule. Du Fu seems to be cautiously committing to Daoist values in his elaborate praise of the temple; he is also courting official patronage.

Here the old house still stands
next to the choked pond

no longer the lively site
where muses came to visit

this place was hard to reach
you had to thread your way

and he'd not ask you back
unless you brought a poem

I hang around to hear
aged neighbors reminisce

then we all grow silent
gaze at the wasted landscape

that big old tree's still standing
brave as a famous soldier

though when the sun goes down
the wind keens in the leaves.

(HUNG 7.) The villa was near Luoyang, and the owner was a friend of the poet's
grandfather. One of the owner's (or Song's) brothers was a distinguished general,
which probably explains the tree reference near the end of the poem.

8. VISITING THE FENGXIAN MONASTERY

I walked around the grounds
in the company of monks

and now they've put me up
to spend a quiet night

the stillness of the valley
is itself a kind of music

the moonlight feels more radiant
filtered through the forest

the cliffs of Heaven Gap
tower toward the stars

I sleep among cold clouds
that chill my dampened clothes

the early prayer bell sounds
as I begin to rouse

is my soul awake
so it may match my senses?

(HUNG 8.) The monastery is part of Longmen, the Buddhist cave-chapel complex near Luoyang. It remains famous for the Buddhist sculpture carved in the rocks. The river there runs between two high cliffs, hence the nickname "Heaven Gap." Although raised in the values of Confucianism and deeply committed to them, Du Fu is clearly expanding his horizons to include Daoist and Buddhist values.

I was in the Eastern Capital
for two whole years

and saw a lot of politics
and dirty tricks

a country boy
I long for vegetables

not for the meat and fish
on the tables of the rich

I need some rice
traditionally prepared

to give me back
my health and color

but I'm too broke
to stock a proper larder

that's why I haven't turned away
to live among the mountains

———

You were a member of the court
an honored man

but you have left it now
to find some peace and quiet

you're visiting these regions
the same as me

now both of us can forage
for precious herbs!

(HUNG 9.) Written in 744, when Du Fu was thirty-two. Li Bai (Li Po) was eleven years older. When they met, Li had been dismissed from the emperor's service and was talking about taking up farming. Du Fu imagines emulating this retirement, but notes that that would require some personal wealth; the emperor, in dismissing the troublesome Li Bai from court, had paid him off handsomely. Du Fu here refers both himself and his high-living friend to the ideal of the hermit, the scholar-poet who retires from government office to meditate and write.

1

I came to find you here this spring
among these greening mountains

whack whack of a distant axe
otherwise just huge quiet

I crossed fast mountain brooks
still rimmed with snow and ice

I climbed past Stone Gate cliffs
to seek you out at sunset

when you glimpse gold and silver
you can just ignore them

you hobnob with the deer
and learn their harmless ways

we walk so far into the woods
that we almost get lost

as free of care as empty boats
drifting with any current.

2

The hermit Zhang
always makes me welcome

tells me to spend the evening
stay the night

carp swim slowly
in his clear pool

deer call out
from the deep spring grass

he pours me cups
of vintage wine

his pears
come from his own trees

it's a steep climb
up to his place

but I come home high
without a care in the world.

(HUNG 10.) Written in the spring of 745. Hung does not translate the second poem. Stone Gate was near the city where Du Fu was living. See the next poem as well.

The autumn water's clear
you see down very deep

a way
to purify your spirit

wise government officials
take time off from their duties

climb on their horses, ride
out to these tangled woods

here are two of the best
a pair of precious jewels

they've brought along a meal
and spared no expense

we eat and watch the twilight
listening in bliss to flutes

even the dragon, deep under water,
wants to join the music.

(HUNG 11.) The prefects who visited the poet, one a magistrate the other a prosecu-
tor, presumably did so in the autumn of 745.

Autumn again and you and I
are thistledown in the wind

we haven't found
what Ge Hong found—

the fabulous elixir
that makes a man immortal

I drink, I sing,
my days are passed in vain

poets are proud and disgraceful
and nobody knows quite why.

(HUNG 12.) This and the following poem celebrate a time of friendship and close
association between the two poets before Du Fu's decision to go west to the capital
again. For Ge Hong, see also poem 89.

Each of Li Bai's lines
is very beautiful

something like Yin Geng,
a poet I've always loved

we have come visiting
among these Dongming hills

and I declare I love Li Bai
the way I would a brother

it's autumn, we get drunk
and share a bed to sleep it off

daily walks
sometimes holding hands

looking for a place
that has some peace and quiet

we've come to see our friend
the scholar of the suburb

as soon as we enter the gate
we're filled with admiration

the young attendant
is so handsome and polite

———

At sundown we hear mallets
pounding the laundry

above this ancient city
hang low banks of clouds

we sing our favorite song
"Evergreen Citron's Great"

do government officers ever retire
for love of vegetable soup?

let's lose all interest in
matters of rank and power

let's let our thoughts and feelings
fly across distant oceans!

2. Back at the Capital, 745–750

Too young to take up the hermit's life and too ambitious to be bohemian in the way Li Bai was, Du Fu returned to the court and capital, Chang'an, where he had previously failed the examination. No doubt he hoped to find a government post. Another exam opportunity presented itself in 747, but nobody passed because it was politically expedient to say that the emperor had not overlooked anyone of talent. The slight to an already established and admired poet was considerable. It left Du Fu seeking patronage, without much success, while he lingered in the capital. He talks often of retiring to a quiet life, probably without any very serious intention. But he was growing steadily in strength and skill as a poet.

Here in my study
I've spent the day alone

all day my thoughts
keep coming back to you

I ponder
our splendid friendship

and the excellence
of all your songs and poems

it's cold and windy here
my clothes are fairly shabby

I know that you're still out there
searching for that elixir

I'd like to get up from this desk
and set right out to visit you

remember how we thought
we could be fellow hermits?

(HUNG 14.) *that elixir:* As a Daoist, Li Bai would be interested in the pursuit of immortality through alchemy. Du Fu is either teasing him about that or just acknowledging their differences, the one a Confucian (in the main), the other more of a mystic, drawn to Daoism and Buddhism.

What a night this is—
old year out, new one in

long watch, bright candles
none of their light wasted

here in the local inn
what pastimes do we have?

we can throw dice
to keep ourselves amused

one man leans across the table
begging for five to come up

another rolls up his sleeves
before he throws and loses

all the politicians
roll dice too, and lose

but an accidental meeting
just might bring good fortune

don't laugh at that!
remember that nonentity, Liu Yi,

penniless
and willing to risk millions!

(HUNG 15.) New Year's Eve (January 25), the year probably 746.

I know no poetry to equal his
his mind must be unique

freshness of Yu Xin
Bao Zhao's delicacy

as I watch the trees leaf out
here, north of the Wei

he's probably gazing at sunset
there, east of the Yangzi

when can we share
a pot of wine again

talk on and on about poetry
until it's nearly daybreak?

(HUNG 16.) Written in the late spring of 746. Li Bai had just moved to the south-eastern coast. Yu Xin was a distinguished poet of the sixth century, an official of the Southern Liang court. Bao Zhao was a fifth-century poet, noted for his poems on solitude and landscape.

18. ANSWER TO A LETTER FROM
MY BROTHER ABOUT THE FLOODS

The yin and yang of our existence
produced this storm and rain

water comes rushing down
from countless high ravines

they say the Yellow River
has burst its usual boundaries

I hear the flooded plains
stretch almost to the sea

every official tries to cope
every district reports disaster

and you, assistant magistrate
in one such flooded district,

no doubt have tried your best
to check the spreading flood

your letter that came two days ago
talked of repairing dykes and levees

you wished that you had help
from crocodiles, turtles,

or magical crows and magpies
the way old stories say

the farm crops south of Yan
are lost this year, completely

even the weeds of Ji
lie under water

snails and clams
around the city walls

snakes and maybe dragons
swim in every pool

I imagine mountain passes
half filled with water

mountains sticking up
like little islands

villages gone
just the treetops showing

ten thousand boats
useless beneath the sky

———

As for me
I am a floating twig

seeking the eastern sea
and the peaches of immortality

well, I will cast my line
and hope to catch

some kind of turtle for you
or maybe even a sea-monster.

———

(HUNG 17.) Probably written in the autumn of 746. Hung's translation of the full title: "A Letter from My Brother Tells of the Long Rain and the Flood of the Yellow River. As an Assistant Magistrate, He Is Worried About the Ruin of the Dykes Under His Charge, and I Send This Poem to Reduce His Anxieties." The letter may have had a public function, to make sure Du's brother didn't get blamed for events that were beyond his control.

He Zhizang rides his horse
like someone trying to steer a boat

walking in his sleep,
he might fall down a well.

*

Prince Ruyang drinks three gallons
before he goes to court

but a brewer's cart goes by
and he starts to salivate—

the government post he'd like?
Prince of the Royal Wine Spring.

*

Ten thousand coins a day
our junior minister spends

on drinks he drinks the way
a whale takes in the ocean

and yet he claims to be
fastidious and choosy.

*

Cui is young and handsome
a carefree individual

he lifts his cup to toast
the wide blue sky

you'd think he was a jade tree
standing there in the wind.

*

Admiring the Buddha
embroidered on a cloth

Su Jin has vowed to be
a vegetarian

but he has lots of lapses
whenever he gets drunk!

*

Li Bai will write you a hundred poems
if you pour him a gallon

he'll fall asleep in a wine shop
in the midst of the busy market

when he was asked to board
the emperor's new barge

he said, "I'm very sorry,
I'm off to drink some wine."

*

Slip three cups of wine
to calligrapher Zhang Xu

and even in front of dignitaries
he will tear off his cap

and use his brush and paper
to draw a group of clouds.

You need to give Jiao Sui
a minimum five gallons

just to wake him up
so he can dazzle all of us

discussing some philosophy
debating points of theory.

(HUNG 18.) Teasing homage to some drinking companions in Chang'an. He Zhizang was nicknamed "crazy" and was a good friend of Li Bai, said to have given him the nickname of "banished immortal." He is said to have had an openhearted love of the lower classes. Li Bai, who was of course elsewhere, is probably included because he was famous for his love of wine. The inclusion of Su Jin, who died some years before, has puzzled commentators as well. Hung suggests a slip of the pen or a corruption of the text. But Du Fu may have been pressing the idea of gods or immortals, mixing the present and absent, living and dead.

Shen and his brother,
lovers of nature,

took me along
for a sail

but the world
turned strangely dark

and the waves
began to break like glass

the boat ran loose
in a crystal chaos

and I, for one, suffered
a hundred fears

what about whales?
what about crocodiles?

what if the wind and waves
engulf our boat completely?

———

The weather starts to clear
and the boatmen get to work

our hosts pitch in as well
unfurl the bright sail

the oars sing their song
geese and gulls rise up

let's have a little music
to welcome the blue sky back

poles and ropes will not
measure this water's depth

as it stirs the water lilies
washing the leaves and blossoms

———

As we come to the lake's middle
we see in its dark depths

the southern mountains, mirrored
upside down in the water

here and there a quiver
as if the mountain moved

maybe our boat will collide
with a high mountain temple

maybe the moon will swim
out of the mountain pass

———

I'd like a black dragon
to offer us a pearl

as the spirit of the waters
governs the movement of sea-beasts

let the water princess and mermaids
venture out to dance

among the lights that flicker
green banners, silver poles

———

There's still a mild fear that
we'll have another thunderstorm

who knows what kind of future
Providence has in store?

youth gives way as it must
to realities of age

joy and sadness take turns
in a dance we don't control.

———

(HUNG 19.) This famous lake was twenty miles southwest of the capital. The variable weather may be meant to reflect the unstable political climate as well.

A flick of the hand
and it's rain or storm

wherever I look
change and fickleness

the old ideal of friendship
as loyalty and permanence

has turned into dirt
under our feet.

(HUNG 20.) Bitterness provoked by the climate of court politics in the capital?

He shakes his head
he will not stay

he'll follow east-going clouds
until they reach the sea

while the rest of us back here
read and admire his poems

he'll drop his fishing line
among the coral reefs

—————

Cold spring, gray sky,
gloomy weather

he'll cross deep mountains,
vast marshes,

keeping the dragons and serpents
off, away in the distance

in a cold spring, amid bright winds,
the world lit by sunset

maybe some goddess will use
her chariot of clouds

to help him find the way
to bliss and carefree living

—————

Ordinary people
cannot sense

that he has immortality
in his bones

loving him so much
we're desperate to keep him

have we forgotten wealth and fame
are dew in morning grass?

———

Only Cai, that fatalist,
counsels us with his silence

he chooses this fine evening
to spread a feast outdoors

I put my lute away
the moon watches sadly

I'll hope he'll write me letters
over all that distance

and in the south, seeking Yu's cave,
if he should meet Li Bai

maybe he will say, "Du Fu
asked for you and hopes all's well."

———

(HUNG 21.) Like Du Fu, Kong had failed the imperial exam and, disgusted by the
political corruption, was determined to relocate. The farewell is poignant because
Du Fu and his friends understand the reasons for parting, and their sympathy
makes them take Kong's part. Yu was a legendary ruler who is said to have deposited
all his books in a cave. The lute is technically a *qin*, a stringed instrument much
favored by poets. Hung translates the full title of this poem as "Farewell to K'ung
Ch'ao-fu [Kong Chaofu], Who, on the Pretext of Illness, Is Leaving for the South-
eastern Coast. Please Show This to Li Po [Li Bai]." (From now on I will change
Hung's spellings to Pinyin without noting the variations.)

1

How nice to board the barge
as the sun meets the horizon

the breeze picks up
the water ripples

we sail past groves
of thick bamboo

and anchor in the cool
of water lilies

the young men mix
some icy drinks

the girls are slicing
lotus roots

but the clouds right overhead
grow black

rain makes me rush
my poem.

2

The shower wets the benches
we were sitting on

the wind blows hard
and rocks the boat

the southern girls'
red skirts drenched

the northern beauties
seem to have ruined their makeup

the mooring line
saws and cuts the willow

the barge's curtains are soaked
from breaking waves

our going home
will be wet and chilly

as if we were having autumn
right in the heart of summer.

(HUNG 22–23.) Hung's version of the full title: "Summer Outing at Changpa Creek with Young Aristocrats and Geishas: Rain Came Toward Evening (Two Poems)."

This old park
is wide and spacious

uninterrupted acres
of soft green grass

our noble young host has picked
the highest knoll for a picnic

flat rivers in the distance
shine like wine

slurping, we drink
from wooden ladles

joking, we gallop around
on saddled horses

———

Spring is reflected
in Princess Pond

drums thunder
from the emperor's walled road

we pass the palace gates
open wide to the sunshine

at the Meandering River
we're met by chariots and silver plates

we watch as dancers' sleeves
almost touch the water

we follow the melodies
spiraling up to the clouds

———

I remember getting drunk
every year at this time

but now I get sad
before I get drunk

my thinning, graying head
is poor and useless

I seem to forfeit everything
in some kind of drinking game

the great court has no use
for this unlucky scholar

where's the next mouthful coming from?
God knows

the party will end
and what will become of me?

here amid this vastness
I stand alone and chant my poem.

(HUNG 24.) The mix of splendid partying and somewhat justified self-pity in this poem makes a good summary of the Chang'an years, with their association with the brilliant court on the one hand and the frustration of not getting an official appointment on the other. Du Fu's poems were apparently admired, but that never translated into consistent patronage or financial security. The poem is dated 748 or 749, so Du Fu was around thirty-seven years old.

3. War and Rebellion, 750–755

*Within five years of Du Fu's time in the capital, the political situation
begin to shift in ways that would affect his poetry as well as his life.
The great rebellion of An Lushan did not break out until 755, but it
was preceded by defeats in border wars against Arabs and Tartars,
and the decline of the dynasty's power in Central Asia no doubt
strengthened the internal forces of discord that erupted in the rebel-
lion. What is significant about Du Fu's part in this is a sudden widen-
ing of sympathy and attention. During these years he married and
started a family, giving him a new set of responsibilities. Friendships
among writers and scholars, parties, and letters to family and friends
were still important to him, but he was suddenly aware, for example,
of the sensibilities of military conscripts and the plights of their fami-
lies. He let them speak for themselves in his poems, perhaps inspired by
similar poems Li Bai had written. Eventually he was himself a
refugee, with personal hardships to report, but well before that he had
begun to show an awareness of the full spectrum of his society, and the
consequences of its political and military upheavals, a breadth of sym-
pathy that has endeared him to generations of readers.*

The war carts creak
horses whinny

armed with their bows and arrows
the soldiers pass

parents, wives, and children
line the road to wave good-bye

the cloud of dust they raise
obscures the Xiangyang Bridge

the families clutch at the soldiers' clothes
and interrupt the march, stumbling,

their crying
rising to the clouds

—

Ask the soldiers and they'll tell you—
"Our lots were drawn again

some of us were first conscripted
when we were just fifteen

sent north to guard the Yellow River
now we're forty and headed to the west

back then the village elders honored us
now we come home with white hair

and then they ship us out again
to where the blood is lapping like a sea

the emperor wants to expand his realm
though back where we come from

whole villages are overrun with weeds
while women try to work the farms

and the fields are a tangled mess at harvest
watercourses choked, crops gone

soldiers from the mountains are good fighters
so they are driven on like dogs and birds

it's good of you to ask about us
but do we really dare complain?

here it is bitter winter
and the Guanxi troops have not returned

tax-gatherers go back and forth
but where will the taxes come from?

it makes us question whether
there's any sense in having sons

daughters can marry neighbors
boys seem born to die in foreign weeds

have you seen how the bones from the past
lie bleached and uncollected near Black Lake?

the new ghosts moan, the old ghosts moan—
we hear them at night, hear them in rain."

(HUNG 29.) A remarkably realistic and subversive look at the effect on ordinary lives
of the government's military and tax commitments. Guanxi was the Western Pass.
Written around 750 (and startlingly contemporary in the twenty-first century).

I

We pack and leave with heavy hearts
heading out to the frontier

the government's set a deadline
deserters will be punished

the empire isn't big enough?
does it have to extend its boundaries?

we march away from our parents' love
shoulder our weapons and swallow our tears.

2

There goes the village elder
who rounds up the recruits

and here I am, packed up
and heading for the front

whether I live or die
I'm going into battle

take it easy, officer
I'm doing as I'm told

maybe out there on the road
I'll meet a friend

who can take back a letter
to those at home

I doubt I'll see them anymore—
we don't even get to die together.

3

Trying out bows we pick the taut ones
choosing arrows we pick the longest

engaging with the enemy
we shoot their horses first

capturing them
we try to begin with their leader

there have to be limits to killing
a country has to have boundaries

it's enough to repel an invasion
why pile up the casualties?

4

The barbarians dared to assault our fort
the air was filled with dust for miles

we waved our swords around
and they collapsed and ran

we caught their famous chief
and made him prisoner

we brought him to the headquarters
a rope around his neck

but this was just one victory
we still must serve our time.

(HUNG 30–33.) From a group of nine poems, obviously following up on the success
of the previous poem. Hung numbers these 1, 4, 6, and 8.

1

I've never been down the road
that leads to South Pond

now I know it lies beyond
Chang'an's Fifth Bridge

the garden there is famous—
next to the green waters

bamboos growing wild
reach toward blue skies

I love secluded spots
happy to be invited

and I'll ride any distance
to visit such retreats.

2

I like these tall bamboos
that grow around the hut

those flowers on the rustic fence
that glow as the sun sets

the puddle might be deep enough
to drown a horse

those thick wisteria vines
twist and wind like snakes

but what's the good of writing
this poetry and prose?

wouldn't it be better
to move to the woods and hills?

I suddenly think about selling
my entire library

so I can buy a hut
and move out here.

3

The yard's tall trees
almost brush the clouds

books piled on beds
nearly reach the ceiling

this is one general
who doesn't care for war

all his children have been taught
to read and write

I wake from a little wine-doze
to feel a light breeze blowing

we listen to some poems
now it's peaceful midnight

the climbing vines make shadows
that stripe our robes

outside a chilly moon
scatters shards of whiteness

4

Sadness invades
our quiet thoughts

we can't stay long
and must return

we leave by the gate
and follow the water

we turn and see behind us
piled white clouds

I have to laugh at myself
always courting the powerful

does anyone like the poems I write
after drinking the wine of the rich?

the only thing that makes sense
is the time spent with my friends

and I will come here often
whether it rains or shines.

(HUNG 35–38.) From a group of ten poems, probably written around 751. Hung's translation of the full title is "Visiting General He's Country Villa with Professor Zheng Qian (Ten Poems)." Zheng Qian was a famous scholar whom Hung describes as "perhaps the most talented and learned man of the time." The emperor had created a new position and office for him. Du Fu obviously feels that He and Zheng represent better company than some of the courtiers whose patronage he had been seeking. The kind of recognition that Zheng received continued to elude Du Fu.

It's best to watch the year depart
with members of the family

singing songs
drinking pepper wine

out in the stables
nervous horses make a racket

the crows are rousted from the trees
by all the torches and lanterns

tomorrow I leave
my fortieth year

my life has started to race
downhill, toward its evening

and what is the use of caution
the value of restraint?

better to put my cares aside
and just get drunk.

(HUNG 39.) Du Wei was a distant cousin. Families celebrated New Year's Eve by staying up and burning lots of lights to ward off evil spirits. They counted themselves a year older on the next day. Thus, counting from his birth in 712, Du Fu figures that he is completing his fortieth year.

1

I wrote to inquire about the bamboos
growing by the eastern bridge

and the general wrote back:
"Get on your horse and come right now

make my house yours
sleep, and have pleasant dreams"

an oriole snatches a falling blossom
thinking it might be a butterfly

an otter roils the brook
pursuing a fish

a perfect place for country folk—
how fine to come back here and rest!

2

Good to drink tea
in this spring breeze

at sunset, I ink my brush
on the terrace's stone balustrade

sit down and write a poem
on a wutong leaf

the kingfisher perches to sing
on a bamboo clothes rack

the dragonfly lands and clings
to my fishing line

now that I've seen what it means
to have some peace and quiet

I plan on coming back
again and again.

3

Whenever I come
I'll stay overnight

I think they would let me
spend a whole year!

I've been stumbling around in my life
it's getting later and later

all those longings
to find my own hermitage

if I could just have a pension
go back to my village, maybe own a farm

but all my plots and plans
keep coming to nothing

I sit with my untouched wine cup
lost in sadness and thought.

(HUNG 40–42.) Written in spring 752. Hung speculates that because Du Fu switches
from the ideal of a hermitage to the ideal of owning a farm in this poem, he was
either newly married or on the verge of marrying. From now on his thoughts of
retreat will envision a wife and family rather than a hermit's solitude.

Up here it's almost as though
we stand astride the sky

a fierce wind
never ceases blowing

and since we human beings
are never free from fear

climbing this high may well
stir up a few new terrors

this religion teaches
that the external world

needs to be distrusted
if ever we're going to know peace . . .

we peer through the carved reliefs
depicting serpents and dragons

impressed by all the supports and beams
that hold up this pagoda

———

Overhead I can count
the seven stars of the Dipper

and imagine I hear the noise
of the Milky Way as it flows

the sun's been pushed below
the westernmost horizon

a clear autumn moon
is trying to rise in the east

because of clouds we see only
shreds of the great mountain

the clear river and the muddy one
mix together and are lost

down below you can't see much
because of all the mist

how can we even be sure
that this is our great empire?

———

Facing the sad and misty grave
of the great Emperor Shun

I call on him to wake
but that isn't going to happen

the Fairy Queen who might help
is off by the Jade Lake

drowning her sorrows in drink
watching another sunset

the yellow cranes depart
I think they won't return

we hear their plaintive calls
where can they find shelter?

and those geese we watched fly off
into the setting sun?

each one of them was searching
for some food.

(HUNG 44.) Written in the autumn of 752. Hung's translation of the full title: "Climbing the Pagoda of Mercy and Grace with Several Gentlemen." The others were all poets: Gao Shi, Xue Ju, Cen Shen, and Chu Guangxi. All of them wrote poems, and the poems of four of the five are still extant, according to Hung. He points out that Du Fu's poem is probably suffused with political meanings. The empire is obscured, the mixed rivers (the clear Wei and the muddy Ching) may represent confusion about standards and values, and the dead and sleeping emperor from the past who won't wake up is also the present one, neglecting his realm. The geese and cranes probably represent the worthies leaving the capital, like Du Fu and his four friends. Rewi Alley's version of this poem, "On Climbing the Big Pagoda in Changan," is, I think, quite effective.

1

The river, looking bleak,
reflects the autumn sky

bits of lotus and chestnut
drift along on its surface

I'm wandering slowly
into my empty old age

I watch the sand and pebbles
stirring along the shoreline

hearing a lone swan call
in search of other swans.

2

I sing what comes to me
in ways both old and modern

my only audience right now—
nearby bushes and trees

the elegant houses stand
in an elegant row, too many

if my heart turns to ashes
that's all right with me

dear brother, little niece,
please stop this crying.

3

I think I'll stop questioning Heaven
about this life of mine

I'm lucky to have two farms
out beyond Du village

and a chance to settle
close to the southern mountains

I'll go around dressed like a peasant
riding an old horse

and spend my time with Li Kuang
watching him shoot tigers.

(HUNG 45.) Meandering River wound through the southern half of Chang'an and
then became a lake with expensive vacation houses along its shore. That is the set-
ting for this poem. The lake and river are more or less abandoned for the season. At
the end Du Fu imagines himself associating with a legendary Han dynasty general,
Li Kuang, who mistook a rock for a tiger and shot it with his bow and arrow. Hung
(who translates only the third part of this three-poem sequence) suggests this may
be an allusion to Du Fu's friendship with General He.

Third day of the third month
a freshness in the air

on the banks of Chang'an's winding river
many gorgeous women

regal bearing, distant manner
warm smiles for each other

immaculate complexions
mostly perfect figures

dressed in embroidered silk
glittering in the sunlight

depicting golden peacocks
and silver unicorns

what do they wear on their heads?
kingfisher ornaments, jade earrings

what do they wear on their backs?
close-fitting pearl-trimmed capes

among them the emperor's relatives
Lady Guo and Lady Qin

now delicacies are served—
purple camel-hump steak, in celadon cauldrons

whitefish, raw,
on crystal plates

but they are already sated
their chopsticks sit unused

elegant shredded morsels
lie untouched

attendants come cantering from the palace
stirring up no dust

the imperial kitchens keep sending out
the rarest delicacies

there's music as well, drums and flutes
poignant enough to raise ghosts

and guests and retainers, enough
to prove the host's importance

and here he comes, quite slowly
riding along on horseback

he dismounts at the pavilion
walks on embroidered cushions

willow catkins fall like snow
cover the white duckweed

a bluebird flies away
carrying a red napkin

don't get too close to this prime minister
his vast power might scorch you

you don't want a man like that
to turn on you in anger!

(HUNG 48.) A mixture of fascination and disgust, portraying the extravagance of the
imperial court and especially the power of the prime minister, Yang, whose sister
was the emperor's concubine. The ladies Guo and Qin were her sisters. Hung sug-
gests a date of April 10, 753, for this poem.

1

All this steady rain
has killed the vegetation

down by the steps a few last flowers
still manage to bloom

putting out leaves on sturdy stalks
blossoms bright as golden coins

but the cold wind's rising
blowing keenly on them

they cannot last, I know,
or stand the season's passing

I watch them from my room
scratching my white head

feeling a little sad
as I take in their fragrance.

2

Wild winds and steady rains
have muddled the autumn season

cloud over all, over
seas and wildernesses

days so dark
you can't tell a horse from an ox

the clear river and the muddy one
are now indistinguishable

the grain heads grow fungus
millet turns black and rots

the farmers and the peasants
bring no produce, no good news

in the city you sell your bedding
for a day's supply of rice

think yourself lucky to have
some food at a bargain price.

3

Imagine a poorly dressed scholar
here in the capital city

home behind closed doors
keeping an empty house

outside the weeds are a jungle
where wet children run and play

and the rain brings whistling wind
and cold sooner than usual

the geese flap wet wings
and cannot fly high or far

it seems as if all this autumn
we've never seen the sun

puddles and mud, we ask
when will the earth be dry?

(HUNG 53.) Hung includes only the second poem. The autumn of 754 saw sixty days
of nonstop rain. Note the poet's concern for the widespread social hardship this
caused.

Oh good, I don't have to be
police commissioner at Hexi!

it would have been backbreaking
supervising all those beatings

I'm an old man, I can't
rush around, bustle, and strut

but the job they've given me now
at Palace Guard headquarters

won't take too much time
it will pay for my wine

and allow me to go on
writing these crazy poems

so no more thoughts about retirement
back in the hills of home

I turn my back on that
and set my face to the wind.

(HUNG 58.) An extraordinary combination of self-mockery, relief, and irony. All of his aspirations for high office have come down to a fairly humiliating outcome: Du Fu had been offered a post as police commissioner of Hexi. The work would be "backbreaking" in two senses: he would be bowing constantly to superiors, and he would be supervising the beatings of common people. He turned it down. He then was offered a minor job in the office of the commandant of the crown prince's palace guard, without almost any real duties. He accepts it wryly and writes this poem to commemorate the end of both his career aspirations and his dream of retiring to a hermit's life.

Imagine a man in commonplace clothes,
advancing years,

impractical and even stupid,
struggling on

he wanted to rank with sages
instead he has white hair and failure

he'll stick with his goals, though, until
they close him into his coffin

a poet who writes from the heart,
anxious about the poor

for which his fellow scholars laugh at him!
well, I will not stop singing

even though I dream
of traveling far away

I have to think the emperor still cares
about this realm of his

the sunflower turns to the sun
that is its very nature

the ant seeks security
retreats to its own burrow

why should it imitate the whale
trying to swallow the seas?

but oh I am sick of begging
whining about my obscurity

I know it all ends in dust
and I think about famous hermits

the only things that relieve my heart
are poetry and drinking

———

Year's end, the grasses withered
a great wind scouring the high ridges

in bitter cold at midnight I set out
along the imperial highway

sharp frost, my belt snaps
my fingers are too stiff to tie it

around dawn I pass
the emperor's winter palace

army banners against the sky
the ground tramped smooth by troops

thick steam from the hot green springs
imperial guards rub elbows

cabinet ministers live it up
the music drifts through the wintry landscape

the hot baths here are for important people
nothing for common folks

the silk the courtiers wear
was woven by poor women

while soldiers beat their husbands
demanding tribute

of course our emperor is generous
he wants the best for us

we have to blame his ministers
when government is bad

plenty of good people at the court
must be especially worried

when they see the palace gold plate
carted off by royal relations

women like goddesses are dancing inside
all silk and perfume

guests in sable furs
music of pipes and fiddles

camel-pad broth is served
with frosted oranges, pungent tangerines

behind those red gates
meat and wine are left to spoil

outside lie the bones
of people who starved and froze

luxury and misery a few feet apart—
my heart aches to think about it!

———

But now I must go on
to cross the Wei and Jing

the ferry landing has been moved
because of floods

one bridge is still intact
above the surging waters

thinking ahead to my wife
trying to cope with this weather

desperate to be with my family
I arrive at last to learn

my little son has died
probably from sheer hunger

and I stand and weep in the street
the neighbors crowd round me, weeping

my shame overwhelms me, a father
who couldn't feed his family

I who have never paid taxes
never been conscripted

I realize I've had an easy life
and I think again of the poor

losing their farms, sons sent to war
no end to their griefs

till my sorrow becomes a mountain
whose peak I cannot see.

(HUNG 59.) Written in 755, on the eve of the rebellion. Du Fu had settled his family
in Fengxian and had made several journeys back and forth to the capital. This
record of one of them represents a new departure in his poetry. He is quite direct in
his criticism of the court's luxury. His fellow feeling for the poor, which his courtier
friends have apparently mocked, is explicitly connected here with his own grief at
losing his child. He feels that his ambition has been self-destructive. No poem of
this kind existed in Chinese poetry before this; it is more personal, more searching,
and more comprehensive than anything that preceded it.

4. Trapped in the Capital, 756–758

The success of the rebellion and the flight of the royal family from Chang'an soon led to a rebel takeover of the city. Du Fu felt he must move his family farther north, an ordeal that is recorded in poem 56, "The Pengya Road." He then, while trying to return and perhaps join the emperor, found himself in the hands of the rebels and forced to stay in the capital. He seems to have had freedom of movement within the city but no means of leaving it; he could not cross the rebel lines and rejoin his family. This situation produced some of his most moving and best-known poems.

Tonight
in this same moonlight

my wife is alone at her window
in Fuzhou

I can hardly bear
to think of my children

too young to understand
why I can't come to them

her hair
must be damp from the mist

her arms
cold jade in the moonlight

when will we stand together
by those slack curtains

while the moonlight dries
the tear-streaks on our faces?

(HUNG 63.) As David Hinton notes, this may be the first Chinese poem to address
romantic sentiments to a wife. Expressions of affection were more typically directed
at male friends and courtesans.

The blood of young men from good families
in many different provinces

mixes now with the water
and marsh mud of early winter

under the empty sky
the battlefield is silent

forty thousand dead, they say,
all in a single day

the Mongols return to camp
and wash their blood-black arrows

sing their savage songs
cavort drunk in the marketplace

and the people of this capital face north
their faces streaked with weeping

hoping day and night for reinforcements,
to come and make things right.

(HUNG 65.) Written in Chang'an when news of the defeat of the imperial forces on
November 17, 755, reached the capital.

The ghosts of the newly dead
lament for their lost battles

and I, an aging codger,
mumble my litany of woes

the swirling wind conducts
a mad dance of snowflakes

the clouds, confused by it all,
crowd toward the sunset

what good is this serving ladle
next to an empty wine pot?

the embers in the stove are ashes
their heat is mostly my imagination

no news comes in
from the outlying provinces

no sense in all of this,
no sense!

(HUNG 67.)

Finally some news
from distant Pingyin

tells me my brothers
are all still alive

they had to flee
made a long journey

found food and rest
in some small village

but the fires of war
are burning all around them

on my face new tears
are running down familiar tracks

the plain fact is, I'm old
and have no way to know

whether I'll ever have
another chance to see them all.

(HUNG 68.) In the east, where the poet's brothers were located, the loyalist forces had at first prevailed and then were defeated. In a companion poem to this one, Du Fu tells them he feels like a failure for having done so little to help protect and shelter them.

The state goes to ruin
mountains and rivers survive

spring in the city
thick leaves, deep grass

in times like these
the flowers seem to weep

birds, as if they too
hated separation

flutter close by
startle the heart

for three months
the beacon fires have been lit

a letter from home
is worth a fortune

this white hair is getting sparse
from scratching

almost too thin
to hold a hatpin!

(HUNG 72.) One of Du Fu's most famous poems.

Here it is spring weather, Pony Boy,
and still we are apart

you must be singing with the orioles
happy in the sunshine

while here I am dismayed
to see how fast the seasons change

I can't be there
to watch your growing mind—

I think about the little streams
the mountain paths we'd visit

the wooden gate, the village
among the ancient trees

I start to fall asleep
imagining I see you

as I lean against this railing
the sun warm on my back.

(HUNG 73.) "Pony Boy" was probably about five years old.

I lie awake and watch
the flicker of the lamp

delicate odor of incense
helps to clear my thoughts

mostly filled with darkness
the central hall looms large

sound of a wind chime
tinkling below the eaves

———

The flowers just outside
are all invisible

but I can smell their fragrance
here in the quiet dark

one of the constellations
is setting behind the roof

passing the iron phoenix
fixed at the temple's peak

———

Pretty soon the monks
will start to chant their sutras

the bell calls them to prayer
I stay in bed

before very long I'll have to rise
and walk across plowed fields

facing the dust and wind
facing my fears and griefs.

(HUNG 76.) The full title, as translated by Hung: "Abbot Zan's Cell in the Dayun
Monastery." Du Fu is hiding in the Dayun (Buddhist) monastery in the capital,
probably to avoid being conscripted into the rebel forces. He has a moment of
peace and quiet in the midst of his hardship and anxiety, but it is inevitably brief.
The constellation is Jade String, more or less the same as our Big Dipper.

I remember when we fled the rebels
heading north through danger and hardship

starting out on foot
in the middle of the night

with the moon shining
over White Water Mountain

a very long journey
all of it walking

when we met people on the road
we felt ashamed

now and then
birds sang in the ravines

no one was headed
in the opposite direction

my silly little daughter
bit me in her hunger

afraid that her crying
might attract tigers

I held her mouth against my chest
she wriggled free and cried louder

my son acted as if he knew
what it was all about

but he kept trying to eat
the bitter plums on the roadside trees

ten days we went, half that time
through thunderstorms

struggling to help each other in the mud
with no protection from the rain

the road was too slippery
our clothes were too thin

some days we couldn't cover
more than a couple of miles

our food was wild berries
our shelter was low branches

mornings we crossed wet, slippery rocks
evenings we camped in mist at the sky's edge

we stopped near Tongjia Marsh
before crossing the Luzi Pass

and my friend Sun Zai
took us in

his generosity
reaches to the clouds

we arrived in pitch-dark
they lit the lamps, opened the gates

the servants brought warm water
to bathe our feet

they cut silhouettes and burned them
to call back our frightened spirits

his wife and children
came out to greet us

when they saw how we looked
they burst into tears

my children, exhausted,
had fallen asleep

we woke them so they could eat
from the platters of food

Master Sun Zai, I swear this vow:
I'm your kin and brother forever

your hall was put at our disposal
and we were told to feel at home

in these bad times where do you find
that kind of trust?

it's a year since we left there
the Tartars are still on the rampage

Sun Zai, I wish I had wings
so I could fly

straight to your house
to see you again!

(HUNG 82.) By the time he wrote this poem, Du Fu had escaped from Chang'an and
journeyed west to join the emperor's exiled court in Fengxiang, about a hundred
miles west. Separated from his family for a year, he found himself recalling their
difficult journey north during the first days of the rebellion, and he re-created it in
this poem. He had finally had news of his family's safety, and of the birth of another
child, and he had secured permission for a leave of absence to visit his family. He
had two hundred miles to go, much of it on foot.

5. Reunion and Recovery, 758–759

The trip to be reunited with his family was successful. He wrote about it in the long poem "The Journey North," excerpted here (61), and in "Qiang Village Poems" (58–60). Meanwhile, the rebels were driven out of the capital, and the new emperor, formerly the crown prince, returned in triumph. Du Fu also returned to Chang'an to resume his new post as Reminder or "Omissioner," someone whose duties were to remind the emperor of important precedents and traditions—a post for which the poet, not always a tactful man, was not ideally suited. Moreover, the new government did not have the means to pay official salaries, so times were still hard for Du Fu, who had moved his family to the capital to be with him. There was still much to feel melancholy about.

Wind in the pines
a stream through the gulley

gray rats scamper
in heaps of broken tiles

here is the ruined palace
of some forgotten prince

some parts of it still standing
under this rugged cliff

blue ghost fires flitting
through dank, empty rooms

outside, a washed-out road
and that swift stream

and all these autumn leaves
making a haunting music

their colors only now
starting to fade and fall

just like those lovely women
under the brown dirt

where is their powder and rouge
where is the prince's chariot?

all that remains
is one stone horse on its side

sadness brims up inside me
I have to sit down in the grass

to sing and then to sob
wiping my streaming eyes

all of us on the road
all restless and unhappy

anything but immortal
not very long to live.

(HUNG 85.) Du Fu is about two-thirds of the way through his journey home. As Hung notes, he knew quite well what prince the palace was built for (Prince Taizong, in 646), but it sounded more poetic to say that the owner was forgotten.

I

From mountainous red clouds
looming in the west

a shaft of sunlight
falls on the flat plain

magpies flap and chatter
around the brushwood gate

all this is hugely welcome
to such a tired traveler

my wife and children
are wide-eyed with surprise

they greet me and of course
must wipe their streaming tears

all of us know these times
whirl families in all directions

we know I'm very lucky
to have returned alive

the neighbors climb their walls
to witness our reunion

pretty soon most of them
are blubbering too

night comes
we light some candles

look at each other
wonder if we are dreaming.

2

It's odd to be an old man
and have new joy in life

to cherish little pleasures
amidst the larger woes

my darling son hugs my knees
afraid I'll disappear again

I think about last year
when he and I escaped the heat

lying beneath the trees
that rim the pond

but now there's a north wind blowing
that tells us winter's coming

I have to think about our needs
to face these hundred worries

I hear, at any rate,
the harvests have been good

the wine is being pressed
I'll have enough to drink

to drown bad memories and help
fend off unhappy thoughts.

3

The chickens are making
a terrible ruckus

I chase them into the trees
to make them stop their fighting

and now I hear some guests
knock at the brushwood gate

these are some village elders
asking about my travels

each one has brought a present
we pour the wine they've given us

and they apologize
for its poor quality

they can't grow better grain
without more help with plowing

all their boys have been
conscripted for the war

I write this poem for them
to say their lives have been

just as hard as mine
I see it in their eyes

after I sing it, sighing,
I lift my face to the sky.

(HUNG 86–88.)

Slowly I make my way
across a ravaged country

smoke from hearths is rare
in this deserted landscape

people I meet are wounded
often still bleeding and groaning

I've said good-bye to the flags and banners
and climbed into the hills

here and there places where
troops of horsemen have camped

I leave the plain behind
and the River Jing that crosses it

a fierce tiger rises in front of me
his roar cracks these slate-blue cliffs

autumn's chrysanthemums
are already starting to droop

next to this rocky road
rutted by many carts

as I climb toward the clouds
I find my spirits rising

the world grows simpler now
inviting meditation

and here are wild berries
along with acorns and chestnuts

some red as cinnabar
others black as lacquer

the rains have ripened them
and made them tart or sweet

I think again of my old dream
of living as a hermit

and it seems to me my life
has been one long mistake

———

I've reached some slopes where I can see
the highlands I'm headed for

and mountain peaks spread out
with valleys deep bctwccn them

I hurry toward the river
my servant lags behind me

owls are hooting now
in yellowing mulberry trees

field mice run and duck
in and out of burrows

in the middle of the night we pass
what must have been a battlefield

the cold moon shines
on white and scattered bones

why should a huge army
so suddenly be destroyed

and this whole region
lose half its population?

————

Well, now I'm coming home
from troubles of my own

and with my hair gone white
I wonder if they'll know me

here's my wife at last
wearing a much-patched dress

crying to see me here
sighing like wind in the pine trees

sobbing uncontrollably
like any tumbling brook

and here's my boy, all pale,
the jewel that crowns my life

he turns his back to me
ashamed of his own weeping

I see his dirty feet
he has no shoes or socks

and there are my two daughters
their clothes all patched as well

too small for them, with images
all crazy and mismatched

a dragon and a phoenix
turned upside down for mending

I feel age overcome me
and take to my bed, all nauseous

three days until I'm better
but meanwhile I've brought

a bag of silks to help them
dress against the cold

and some bedding for them
and a few cosmetics

my wife's face takes on color
the little girls' as well

they start to play with makeup
to imitate their mother

they overdo the rouge
and paint on crooked eyebrows

just being with my children
restores my strength and spirits

I'd rather have them pester me
and shower me with questions

than ever have to deal again
with rebels and their ways.

(HUNG 89.) Part of a longer poem in which the first and last parts deal with the polit-
ical situation and Du Fu's uncertainty about taking a leave in such difficult times.
He predicts better times for the dynasty and ends on a note of hope. About the sec-
tion with which this selection ends, A. R. Davis comments: "No similar sustained
description of a domestic scene can be found in earlier Chinese poetry. . . . By this
period in his life he had achieved complete sureness, and he clearly set no limita-
tions to the subject matter of poetry."

1

Every fallen petal
diminishes spring

so the wind showers down a thousand
just to make me sad

I'll keep my eyes
on the ones that remain

and have some wine
whether it's good for me or not

kingfishers nest
in the ruins by the river

a stone unicorn
lies on its side in the park

Nature says, enjoy yourself
and don't waste time

why worry then
about things like rank and office?

2

Daily, after court
I take my clothes to the pawnshop

every night
I come back from the riverbank, drunk

I have an unpaid bill
in every tavern

well, who lives to be seventy
anyway?

butterflies
deep in the flowers

dragonflies
flicking the river's surface

let them all go on—
time and the wind and the light

since we're told not to defy them
let's enjoy them while we can!

(HUNG 103–104.) The capital was retaken and the new emperor installed, amid rejoicing. Du Fu got to rejoin the court and resume his post as Reminder. This lasted about a year, after which he and his friends were effectively banished from court by being given official positions elsewhere; Du Fu was posted to Huazhou to take up an appointment as a commissioner of education. While many of the poems from this Chang'an year are about his work at the court and about the political situation, this meditation next to the Meandering River in the spring of 758 is the most memorable and complex, ranging from some self-criticism and melancholy to a philosophical endorsement of hedonism and detachment.

Middle of August and the heat
is just about unbearable

and who could have any appetite
in all this steam?

at night I lie awake
and worry about the scorpions

and now the flies are getting worse
as summer moves toward autumn

wearing the robes and belts of office
I sit at work and want to scream

and my subordinates
just pile up more paperwork

I stare out the window at the pines
that rim the canyons in the distant mountains

and dream of walking barefoot
across crushed ice!

(HUNG 109.) At the new appointment.

The clouds float off
the way the sun went

the traveler
does not come back

three nights in a row
I dreamed of you, old friend,

you were so real
I could have touched you!

you left in a hurry
but seemed each time to hesitate

I'll bet
you're having a bad journey

storms come up fast
on these rivers and lakes

don't lose your paddle
or fall out of the boat!

leaving, framed in the doorway,
you scratched your snowy head

as if you didn't want to go
didn't know what to do with your sadness

bureaucrats fatten in the capital
while a poet goes cold and hungry

if there is justice in heaven
what sent you out to exile?

ages to come
will warm themselves at your verses

but what reward is that
for your unappreciated life?

(HUNG III.) This is the second of two poems.

66. IN THE CITY ON BUSINESS I MEET ONE FRIEND AND WE SPEND THE NIGHT EATING AND DRINKING AT THE HOUSE OF ANOTHER

A high wind
blows dust through the river districts

travelers pass, hands over eyes
unrecognized

east of the city
I open my eyes

and there, as I tie up my horse
I see Yun Jing!

Let's go see
Liu Hao

it'll be worth the extra trip

———

Taking our hands
he leads us in

lights lamps, pours wine,
sets out dish after dish

"Let's talk all night," he says
"and live it up

and not one word about the war!"

———

The stove burns red
like a tiny dawn

and the moon makes the paper window
shine like rippled silk

a while ago the uproar at the capital
turned the whole world on its head

now winter's over, spring has begun
even around the palace walls

who'd have thought our tracks
would cross again like this?

where has the time gone?
look at the water clock!

and why is life
so full of good-byes?

as we part in the yard
roosters are crowing in the trees

and we cry a little, drunk and happy,
tears threading our cheeks.

(HUNG 114.) Hung's note: "Toward the end of the solar-lunar calendar year, which
would be about the end of January 759, Tu Fu was sent on business 227 miles east-
ward to Lo-yang. On the way he met Meng Yunjing east of the city of Huzheng and
returned with Meng to drink in the home of a friend."

6. On the Move, 759

In the autumn of 759 Du Fu left his official post at Huazhou and moved his family west and then south, first to Qinzhou, more than three hundred miles to the west. After two months they moved on, south this time to Tonggu, another forty-five miles. By the end of the year they were headed to Chengdu, another five hundred miles south. Just why the official post was abandoned seems clear: the poet was sick of his bureaucratic duties, and the political situation, with rebel troops in the area, was very uncertain. Why he chose the western and southern places of sojourn, and why he moved on after a short time in the first two, is a matter of conjecture. Perhaps he hoped for support from friends and relatives in these areas. In any case, all the traveling did not put a constraint on his writing; if anything, it made him more productive.

Garrison drums
stop travel

autumn on the frontier
sound of one wild goose

nightfall—from now on
the dew will be white

this same moon shines
where I grew up

my brothers are scattered
no way to know if they're alive

the letters we send each other
never seem to arrive

and the war goes on and on.

(HUNG 124.) The poet has traveled west, away from the fighting in the east and his scattered brothers. The White Dew season, a subdivision of the lunar-solar calendar, followed the Mid-Autumn Festival.

1

Trouble is part of life—
relying on good advice

I find myself making
this difficult journey

we climb the mountain slowly
fearing the cliffs

we cross a swift river by night
then climb on into the hills

heading west
wondering about the beacon fires

does that mean
we'll come upon more fighting?

2

This monastery
north of the city

was a palace once
belonging to Wei Hsiao

its old stone gate
is covered with moss

the painted hall is now
empty and run-down

a bright moon shines
on dew-heavy leaves

patchy clouds chase the wind
above the River Wei

clear and heartless
it flows east and leaves me sad.

3

A confused heap of mountains·
lording it over

a lonely city
in the valley

no wind here
but the clouds are moving overhead

it isn't night
but the moon's above the pass

why hasn't
that embassy come back?

did they wait for a chance
to kill the rebel chieftain?

I watch the west
for smoke and dust

anxious and looking even older
than I am.

4

I like the beauty
of this rocky valley

the best one around here
I think

birds in pairs
fly into the sunset

one cloud
in a clear sky

the remoteness of all this
is what the natives boast of

plenty of water
plenty of bamboo

I think about settling here
learning to gather healing herbs

although I haven't said so
to my children.

(HUNG 127–129.) Part of a group of twenty miscellaneous poems about the Qinzhou area. The first of these is not included in Hung. Davis comments: "His response to this border city, set among 'ten thousand mountain-folds,' was mixed. The isolation depressed him, although at times he felt exhilaration at the wild scenery." The fourth poem is about the Tonggu valley, where his cousin Du Zuo lived.

Behind the wooden gate
of Ruan's small hermitage

vegetables grow in the garden
that surrounds the house

wet with morning dew
here's a big basket of shallots

that he has sent
without my even asking

the leaves as green as grass
the white jade bulbs

old men can dread the cold
with winter coming on

these will warm my stomach
on many chilly days.

(HUNG 134.) Hung translates the full title as "Thirty Bundles of Shallots from Hermit Ruan Fang on an Autumn Day."

How come you've ended up
here in this distant spot

where autumn winds
already nip us

rain has rotted
chrysanthemums in the courtyard

and frost has felled
half the pool's lotus plants

exile of this kind
is nothing that upsets you

you who contemplate
all of the world's nothingness

fortunate that we've met
and can pass the night talking

as if the full moon
was shining just for us.

(HUNG 135.) For Abbot Zan, see poem 55. This same person, whom Du Fu knew
and was sheltered by in Chang'an, had been exiled to the Qinzhou area. Du Fu
briefly contemplated settling near him.

Such a thin moon!
in its first quarter

a slanting shadow
a partly finished ring

barely risen
over the ancient fort

hanging at the edge
of the evening clouds

the Milky Way
hasn't changed color

the mountain passes
are cold and empty

there's white dew
in the front courtyard

secretly filling
the drenched carnations.

(HUNG 142.) A good example of the simplicity and economy Du Fu could command
by this point.

The autumn air goes on and on
clear and crisp for miles

just a layer of mist
on the far horizon

the distant river carries
the clear sky's image

the city is blurred
by the smoke of a thousand hearths

wind takes a few more leaves
off the thinning trees

sun has just gone down
behind those distant hills

one crane flapping home
takes his time

the woods are already full of crows
roosting for the night.

(HUNG 143.)

I have this feeling
you won't come back from frontier duties

but autumn is here
and I get out the laundry stone

soon you'll feel the cold
the way I feel our separation

I clean your winter clothes
whether I want to or not

send them off to where you're stationed
near the Great Wall

a woman uses all her strength
beating the laundry with a club

maybe if you listen hard
you'll hear it way out there.

(HUNG 144.) The sound of laundry being pounded, often at night, was a frequent detail in poems about melancholy and insomnia. Poems about wives whose husbands were away were also not uncommon. The decision to cast the poem in the voice of such a woman was a more unusual feature, although Li Bai, not surprisingly, had done it first.

77. THE CRICKET

Such a tiny creature
the cricket

how greatly it can move us
with its sad chirp

no longer willing
to live among weeds and roots

it came indoors to join us
living under our bed

making a sound that might cause
a traveler to burst into tears

or keep a wife whose husband's gone
awake until dawn

no human things
guitar or flute

quite match up
to nature's music.

(HUNG 145.)

As I age I seem to grow
lazier and more stupid

more or less unable
to plan ahead

when we're hungry
I ask where crops are ample

and when we're cold
I'm suddenly interested in the South.

———

The weather this November should be mild
in Hanyuan province

not so many trees gone bare
not so many withered plants

all in all, they say,
a most mysterious landscape

I love the name of where we're going—
Chestnut Station—that sounds lucky!

lots of decent farmland
on the plains

and yams enough
to fill your belly

wild honey
gathered from the cliffs

bamboo forests all year round
bamboo shoots to eat

clear lakes
and boats to fish them

a far-off place
for me and my wandering family

but we're committed now

―――

Qinzhou
was on the main highway

connected to all
those human complexities

I got a little tired
of all the socializing

being taken to see vistas
didn't address my problems

the mountain valleys
lack strange rocks

the sandy soil
yields poor crops

none of this satisfies
a poor old man

it's clearly time to leave

―――

The old fort disappears
into the dusk

ravens call
perched on the city walls

we leave at night
with carts

water the horses
at a pond beside the road

overhead a moon
and wilderness of stars

here and there
clouds and mist

this universe
is enormous,

my road goes on and on.

(HUNG 149.) Du Fu was moving his family to Tonggu, to a place called Chestnut Station, by way of Hanyuan province. Hung estimates the total distance of this journey as 137 miles.

1

A wayfarer called Zimei
(me, to be precise),

unkempt white hair
falling around my ears

hungry, out foraging
picking up acorns

dusk on a winter day
mountain ravine

no news from home
on the Central Plains

anyway
I can't go back there

hands numb, skin chapped,
bones and flesh, just half alive

*Oh this first song
is a sad song*

*a bitter wind for me
that comes right down from heaven.*

2

Long-handled shovel
white ash-wood

you're my means
of livelihood

trying to find sprouting yams
under the mountain snow

I tug my coat around me
but it won't cover my shins

I'll go home empty-handed
except for this cursed shovel

and there will be my family
groaning with cold in their empty room

*And oh this second song
is turning into a howl*

*my neighbors will grow sad
just listening!*

3

Brothers
far away from me

all three must be thin
I wonder which is strongest

we roll away from each other
and have no chance to meet

the roads between are long
and choked with the dust of Northern troops

I watch the cranes and geese
fly over, heading east

if I could go with them
and be with you!

Oh third little song sung thrice
you're just as sad

if I die here
how will they gather my bones?

4

My sister lives
in Zhongli District

her husband gone
children young and weak

Huai River's long
with fierce flood dragons

ten years since I have seen her
but how can I see her now?

I have no boat
with which to sail to her

arrows fill the eye
war banners wave

Oh this fourth song,
sung four times through,

may make the monkeys
weep in the forest!

5

Windy hills all round
countless mountain streams

the cold rain hammers
the dead trees drip

yellow weeds and bushes
grow next to the ancient city walls

a white fox runs by
a brown fox stands and watches

I keep wondering
why is my life like this

and why should I spend it
here in this lonely valley?

I wake and pace all night
grappling with my troubles

And oh this fifth song is
sung long!

call for my spirit, it won't come
it's gone home to my native village!

6

In the South there's a dragon
sleeping in his pool

old trees rise there
tangling their twisted branches

leaves turn yellow and fall
the dragon hibernates

poisonous snakes come from the east
how can they do that?

I'd draw a sword but I'm afraid
I could do little good

And oh my sixth song
carries through the air

as the day warms and the stream and valleys
start to come back to spring again.

7

So here I am—
born a man

I've won no fame
and now I'm old

walking the mountain roads
through three long years of famine

the bigwigs in Chang'an are young
competing for wealth and position

deep in the mountains live old men
wise scholars, friends of mine

we talk about old times
and show our scars

And oh my seventh song
ends quietly

as the white sun runs
across the summer sky.

(HUNG 144–147.) As this group of poems makes clear, the move to Tonggu did not turn out well. Characteristically, Du Fu makes bitter but lilting songs out of his poverty, suffering, and depression. But the picture of a shivering man foraging for acorns and yams while missing his brothers and sisters shows his deep disappointment. In the opening song he refers to himself by his sobriquet, Zimei. In the sixth song the hibernating dragon seems to be the emperor and the poisonous snakes the rebels. In the seventh his stocktaking involves his sense that he has not really fulfilled his talents by achieving any kind of significant fame.

A famous wise man
never built a fire in his hearth

another one, it's said
never sat long enough to warm his mat

so here's one hungry, foolish man
who's following their example

it seems I just can't settle
in one place

when I arrived
among these mountains

I reveled in their remoteness
and thought, "I'll rest here quietly"

but now my situation
whether I like it or not

will have me make another trip
that's four in just one year!

I leave this obscure place
with real regret

set out with great uncertainty
on yet another journey

I stop my horses
amid the clouds by Dragon Pool

one last time I admire
the rocks of Tiger Cliff

here where the road forks
friends have come to say farewell

I take their hands in turn
tears brim in my eyes

not that we've had a long acquaintance
leading to deep friendship

but more that an old man
falls easily into sadness

this seemed like a perfect place
for a clumsy, lazy man like me

an ideal place in many ways
to be a hermit

I do not want to leave
I do not want to stay

I turn with shame to watch
the birds among the branches.

(HUNG 158.)

7. Thatched Cottage, 759–762

The next move was farther south, to Chengdu, capital of Sichuan, known as "the Brocade City" and designated as the southern capital. Leaving in late December 759, Du Fu and his family managed the journey of some five hundred miles in about a week, according to Hung. Here the poet would settle and build a house, the famous "Thatched Cottage" (often rendered as "Thatched Hut," but it was more ample than the word "hut" implies), not far from the city and near a monastery where he and his family stayed while the house was being built. Davis comments: "Though he had now reached almost the furthest point of his travels and his homesickness was extreme, he was about to enjoy two or three years of almost happiness." He was also embarking on the last decade of his life.

The late sun
sinking through the trees

brightens up
my traveling clothes

I've come a long way
through variegated landscapes

to this far corner
of our known world

nearly everyone I meet
will be new to me

and I can't think of going home
maybe ever again

this Great River
flows away to the east

like me
it's always moving

Chengdu has city walls
fine houses behind them

the trees are green
even in late winter

I've heard a lot about
this city

listen, there's a sound
of people making music

that doesn't cure
my loneliness!

I turn to look
at the bridge across the river

crows and even sparrows
returning to their nests

how far away
the Central Plains seem now

the crescent moon
does not rise high

the stars have most of the rest of the sky
to compete among themselves

exile and travel
are familiar stories

why should I let them
make me sad?

(HUNG 160.)

88. SITING A HOUSE

By the Flower-Washing River
on the western bank

master of my house, I've chosen
this quiet woods and riverbank

outside the city, well away
from business, dust, entanglements

here where clear water
rinses away a traveler's sadness

too many dragonflies to count
hover and play on the water

two wood ducks swim straight toward me
then dive and disappear

I could go a thousand miles east
riding on my high spirits

skimming along in the shade of mountains
aboard a simple skiff!

(HUNG 162.) The name for the river came from Chengdu's reputation for floral dec-
orations on brocade. The ending refers to an inspired boat journey by Wang Zixian
(fourth century), who remarked that he had come in high spirits and was returning
in exhaustion.

Beyond the smoke and dust
of Brocade City

sits our little river village
eight or nine houses

lotus leaves float
small and round

blossoming wheat stalks
bend toward the ground

now I have a house
in which I can grow old

a farmer who feels remote
from all that happens in the capital

though I wish I could be like Ge Hong
that man of ancient days

who held an office but still went out
in search of life's elixir!

(HUNG 168.) Note the wistfulness at the end, where the poet thinks of Ge Hong (c. 284–c. 364) who had it both ways: holding office and yet ranging the woods to gather cinnabar in search of the elixir of immortality, a Li Bai–like activity. Du Fu has partly accepted his new role, out of governmental affairs, and partly still longs for office.

The river curves
to flow around our village

which holds a secret beauty
on these long summer days

the swallows come and go
among the eaves and rafters

floating, flocked together
gulls sit on the water

my wife creates a chessboard
drawing it on paper

our sons make fishhooks
bending some old needles

sometimes when I am sick
I may require medicine,

but that is really all
this humble person needs.

(HUNG 169.) This and the following four poems (91–94) are vignettes of life in the new place. Of the reference to his asthma in poem 90, Hinton notes that Du Fu had had his house "Qi-sited" (see also poem 88), meaning that a geomancer, a feng shui expert, would have helped plan its positioning so as to afford maximum health, with particular attention to the poet's affliction. Hence also the references to his need for medicines; his garden included medicinal plants and herbs.

Sojourner in the southern capital
I farm these southern fields

sit by the north-facing window
gazing back and feeling sad

better to do what I've done this morning
go boating with my wife

we watch our children in bright sunlight
splash in the clear river

butterflies flying in pairs
chase each other, mating

two perfect lotus blossoms
match on a single stalk

here comes some tea and sugarcane juice
brought down from the house

our earthen pots are just as good
as any made of jade!

(HUNG 170.)

Difficulty breathing—
my old asthma

it's better here
in this new river home

a little distance
from the city's noise and bustle

the fresh air here
seems to strengthen me

and when a guest arrives
at our thatched cottage

my son helps me
adjust my farmer's cap

I show off the young vegetables
I myself have planted

and pick a few to offer
as tokens of our friendship.

(HUNG 171.)

93. RETIREMENT

I rise late and when I get up
check on chores to do

today there aren't any
so I luxuriate

admiring the bamboo's green
against the green of the plain

even the reflection of my cottage
wavering in the river

I'm letting my children get lazy
without a lot of schooling

I'm letting my wife worry
about our perpetual poverty

seems like my life
is a kind of drunken dream

and it must be a month
since I've even combed my hair!

(HUNG 174.)

My thatched cottage stands
just west of Thousand Mile Bridge

this Hundred Flower Stream
would please a hermit fisherman

bamboo sways in the wind
graceful as any court beauty

rain makes the lotus flowers
even more red and fragrant

but I no longer hear from friends
who live on princely salaries

my children are always hungry
with pale and famished faces

does a madman grow more happy
before he dies in the gutter?

I laugh at myself—a madman
growing older, growing madder.

(HUNG 180.) Discussed in my introduction.

Howling madly
a big September storm

took off three layers
of our thatched roof

spreading them on the river
and all along the banks

even high up and hanging
among the branches of the trees

along the ground as well
in all the pools and hollows

and then the boys from South Village
taking advantage of my weak old age

helped themselves to thatch
right in front of me

carrying off armfuls
into the bamboo grove

ignoring my shouts
until my voice was hoarse . . .

I trudge back home, sighing
leaning on my stick

the wind dies down
the clouds are still quite black

they seem to reinforce
the long autumn night

my threadbare quilt
is cold as iron now

my little son sleeping restlessly
has kicked it full of holes

right above my bed
the roof is leaking, there's no dry spot

disrupted sleep again, it's been this way
ever since the Rebellion

huddled up, trying to get through
this cold, soaked night

I dream of a great big house
with maybe a million rooms

shelter for all poor scholars
to make them smile

even in huge rainstorms
unshakable mountain of a house

if such a house sprang up
right before my eyes

my hut could smash and I could freeze to death—
I'd still die happy.

(HUNG 183.) From the autumn of 860. The poem is especially admired for the sentiments at the end, e.g., Hung: "A sick man without shelter thinking of solving the housing problem for the whole world is like a soldier dying on a battlefield dreaming of universal peace."

Congratulations, rain
you know when to fall

and you know quite well
you belong to spring

coming at night, quiet
walking in the wind

making sure things
get good and wet

the clouds hang dark
over country roads

there's one light from a boat
coming downriver

in the red morning
everything's wet

flowers all through Chengdu
heavy and full of rain.

(HUNG 187.) Deservedly a classic.

1

The riverside flowers
are driving me crazy

because there's no way
to describe their effect

I went to see
my neighbor and fellow drinker

he's on a ten-day bender
all I found was an empty bed.

2

Flowers in crowds, shoals, galaxies
swarm and tangle by the river

I don't walk I stagger
spring knocks me out

two things I can still manage
wine and poetry

you flowers
have pity on a white-haired man.

3

A few houses here
where the river is deep and the bamboos quiet

but these flowers
this red and white flirtation

and what can I give
in return?

yo, spring!
have some of this good wine.

4

Over to the east
Chengdu's flowers are lost in smoke

and Hundred Blossom Tower
has it worse

who can afford that place—
wine in gold cups

dancing girls
in plush surroundings?

5

On the other side of the river
here's Abbot Huang's grave

spring light seems drowsy here
leaning against the breezes

a mass of peach blossoms
waiting to be picked

what do I want
a red one or a pink one?

6

Mrs. Huang's garden
flowers engulfing the paths

thousands
weighing the branches

butterflies move pause move pause
it's a dance

and the adorable orioles
know the appropriate music.

7

It's not that I love them so much
I'm likely to die along with them

but I know I'll age more quickly
when they're gone

clusters, don't wither and droop
so quickly

little buds, don't rush it
open slowly!

(HUNG 191–197.) These poems belong to the spring of 761.

1

My sorrow is perfectly visible
to spring, that painted hussy

but she visits my river pavilion
as if it meant nothing at all

encourages the flowers
to open shamelessly

then persuades the orioles
to sing themselves into a frenzy.

2

I planted these peach and plum trees
it's not like they have no owner

my fences are not very high
but they do mark off my property

so what gives spring wind, that thug,
the right to come in at night

and help itself to a few
of my blossoms and their branches?

3

They know my study is small
here below the thatched roof

but the swallows from the river
fly right into it anyway

the mud in their beaks spatters
my *qin* and my best books

they chase the little insects
to bump against my face!

    4

March is long gone
April is half over

how many more spring seasons
can any old man have?

well, stop these thoughts about
life, death, and infinity!

drink what's left of your wine
enjoy it while you can.

    5

Spring's almost over along the river
it breaks my heart to watch it

I walk with my thorn stick
drinking the fragrance of the shore

willow catkins
drift by on the wind

silly little peach blossoms
sail on the river's surface.

    6

Lazy is what I am
I never leave the village

I tell my son to close
the wicker gate this morning

green moss and turbid wine
silence within the pine grove

water as blue as jade, spring breeze
dusk scudding across the landscape.

7

Willow catkins on the path
making a white carpet

lotus leaves on the stream
a string of big green coins

pheasant chicks, invisible
among the bamboo shoots

ducklings on the sand
dozing next to their mother.

8

West of the cottage, mulberry leaves
soft and ready for plucking

ears of wheat on the riverbank
raising their spears again

how many times in one life
can spring change into summer?

I want to drain the wine cup
the lees like honey in the bottom.

9

Just outside my door
frail and slender willows

graceful as the waists
of fifteen-year-old girls

who was it said this morning
"things are the same as ever"?

that wild wind has broken
the willow's longest branch.

(HUNG 198–203.) Hung includes only sections 1, 2, 3, 4, 5, and 7 of "Random Feelings." The personifications of the season in the first section and of the spring wind in the second are unusual tropes for Chinese poetry. The *qin* is the instrument, something like a zither, that has been variously translated as "lute," "harp," or "guitar."

It's when the descending sun
is level with the curtain hooks

that spring along this river
is at its very best

good smells surround the gardens
along the riverbank

a column of smoke from the beach
where boatmen cook their dinners

steadily chattering sparrows
fight to roost in the evening trees

gnats and mayflies swarm
in the air of my front yard

oh cup of cloudy wine
you too are a gift

a sip or two of you dissolves
all my little worries.

(HUNG 205.)

8. More Disruptions, 762–765

The two peaceful years in the thatched cottage were idyllic, though we can easily imagine the poet growing a little restive. In any case, more rebellions were in process, some of them in the very area where he had settled. In 761 his friend Yan Wu had become governor general of the area, but by May 762, when there was a struggle for power in the capital, Yan Wu was called back. Du Fu decided to travel partway with him, and the second of his farewell poems (114) was composed along the way. He speaks of returning, but a revolt had broken out in Chengdu and he ended up in Zizhou, where his family joined him. He was apparently anxious to avoid association with any faction and had to be circumspect about where he went and with whom he associated.

We've come this far together
and now I say farewell

these peaks, empty and blue,
echo our feelings

when will we next lift wine cups
or stroll in moonlight like last night?

you're loved and praised and will be missed
in many prefectures

you've served three emperors
at court and in the provinces

well, I'll go back to my river village
all by myself tomorrow

to finish the years I have left
in solitude and silence.

(HUNG 220.) Yan Wu was in fact greatly delayed on his journey by the spreading rebellion, and Du Fu either didn't get back home or was able to stay there only briefly.

I traveled east
but I kept turning back

took a few steps
and then looked west again

would Chengdu be in ruins now
after the uprising?

was my thatched cottage still intact
beside the Flower-Washing Stream?

————

Here in Zizhou
who's the greatest hero?

it's Vice Prefect Yan
and he is justly famous

he takes me by the arm
opens the wine pots, pours full cups

giddy with wine, we dance with swords
and roar like dragons!

and while his people brush my dusty cap
and feed and water my gray donkey

men in red and purple robes
bring roasts out to us

and on the bronze supports
the candles burn like daylight

———

Later, just the two of us
talk together from the heart

I came to your gate at dusk
and knocked, a stranger

scarcely thinking that I'd fall
straight into this deep friendship

that nothing else
would really matter

my life just filling up
with goodwill and sheer happiness

a friend I could admire
from whom I could take comfort

while the disease of all my wanderings
could drop away from me

and this world's superficial friendships
could cease to matter

too bad we meet in my old age
but better late than never

men such as you exist
mainly among the ancients!

———

(HUNG 223.) Du Fu found good hospitality at Zizhou in the person of the wealthy
vice prefect, Yan, and celebrated it in this poem.

By temperament
I'm very free and easygoing

and living close to nature
truly suits me best

wine pleases me, and watching
the wind in the bamboos

I like to live near a forest
and never far from a spring

war and disorder washed me up
on the riverside in Shu

a good place to recuperate
from my long travel sickness

——

At first we only cleared
a little patch of weeds

then gradually we used
more and more ground

started building the cottage
over two years ago

kept on making additions
right up to this year

I didn't dare
build something elegant

but we had a firm foundation
and a very splendid setting

pavilions and small terraces
shaped to the land's contours

everything open and spacious
and right there next to the river

good friends
were living all around us

we used to go out
in fishing boats on the river

but because there was a war
we seldom made music and we slept lightly

like a dragon that never
settles in one place

or a brown crane
that wings into the sky

from ancient days
the wisest men

have never let conditions
affect their basic freedom

but I'm not much like them
I'm unwise and shortsighted

I couldn't quite foresee
the bind that we got into

———

Now I have to take away
my wife and children

once more we're all exposed
to wind and drifting mist

and while this may be something
we don't really have to do

I must think about my name
and how best to protect it

well, now I'm starting to worry
about my four small pines

what if the weeds
grow up and smother them?

they aren't yet sturdy enough
to manage on their own

maybe the neighbors
will look after them?

(HUNG 224.) Missing the thatched cottage and worrying about who would tend his plants. His concern about protecting his reputation by staying out of rebel-held territories stems from experience and from the examples of friends, like Li Bai.

Here in Sichuan we get word
of the full recovery of the Central Plains

I blubber so much at the news
I soak the clothes I'm wearing

I turn to my wife and children
all our cares are gone!

and like a maniac I start
packing, rolling up all my poems

now we can sing and dance
right here in broad daylight

drink some wine
and then some more

delirious, I want to start for home
the green spring my companion

I'll go out through the great
Yangzi River gorges

on to Xiangyang and finally
be back home in Luoyang!

(HUNG 225.) The An Lushan Rebellion was finally over and it seemed safe to travel east. Du Fu is anxious to see his brothers and his property in the eastern capital. The hoped-for journey was not to occur.

Sitting at dinner, our wandering family
is startled by two swallows

who fly right into the hall
carrying mud in their beaks

it's fair that we should share this shelter
from the unpleasant weather

and pass the time together
fickle as it is . . .

like us you try to raise your children
among the wind and dust

like us you must have come
a long way just to get here

and in the autumn you'll depart
if this world still exists

and we'll be going too, leaving
this strange place behind.

(HUNG 227.) These swallows are treated more empathetically than the ones who
were in poem 106.

Far from home
with farther still to travel

I stop my horse
beside this lonely grave

the earth is wet
as if from recent weeping

the low sky
is full of broken clouds

the two of us used to play *weiqi*
unruffled by bad news

but I have come too late
to present you with my sword

there's nothing here to see
but blossoms falling in the forest

nothing to hear but the song of an oriole
sending me on my way.

(NOT IN HUNG.) Written in the autumn of 763. Fang had been high in the government during the rebellion, but had been exiled for losing key battles to the rebels. The game *weiqi*, sometimes translated "chess," is in fact more like the Japanese *Go*, which originated in China. Fang's friendship with Du Fu went back to the Chang'an days ten years earlier.

The flowers growing around the tower
wound this pilgrim's heart

it's a time, after all, when the empire
is much beset by troubles

but the Brocade River springtime
spread out below is a pure delight

the clouds around Jade Rampart Mountain
will shift and change like history itself

but like a dynasty, the North Star
shines beyond all change

now may the Tibetan marauders
end all their raids and invasions

I'm moved to recall that poor ruler
who nevertheless has a shrine

and as evening comes on before me
I hum a dirgelike folk song.

(HUNG 249.) At the end of this poem Du Fu is recalling an ancient hero who came
to the aid of the last ruler of Shu, Liu Chan. This hero, Zhuge Liang (181–234),
was buried with the last ruler in Chengdu. The folk song was associated with him
as well.

Cool autumn air beside the well
chills the wutong trees

here in the river city, staying by myself,
I watch the candles burn low

I mutter to myself, disconsolate,
the bugles call all night

the moon rides high overhead
and no one else is watching it

unrest goes on, like wind and dust,
and letters never get through

the roads through the passes are deserted
nobody wants to be traveling

ten long years now
I have been displaced

so here I'll roost awhile
upon this peaceful bough.

(HUNG 253.) In 764 Du Fu received an appointment to the military staff of Yan Wu,
who had returned (see poem 114) to govern the province. He put off his plans to
sail east on the Yangzi and settled back in at the thatched cottage. His duties, which
were primarily to help advise and administrate the campaign against Tibetan
invaders, often kept him in the city, as this poem commemorates.

The bamboos rattle in the cold
the sound invades my sleep

the moon above the plains
fills one side of my garden

countless tiny drops
make up this heavy dew

scattered stars
come and go without warning

fireflies signal
back and forth in the dark

birds roosting near the creek
call softly to each other

amid all the ongoing
war and mayhem

I sit up, feeling hollow,
as the clear night wheels past.

(HUNG 257.) A companion piece to poem 121 and one of the most famous insomnia poems ever written. The locale is the thatched cottage, presumably, and the poet's asthma may be part of the explanation for his sleeplessness. I have revised this substantially from the version in my book *Five T'ang Poets*.

1

Farmers are busy everywhere
in the fields beside the river

the springs are full
and the river waters deep

I gaze at earth and heaven
as though I could see for miles

the change of seasons makes me think
I'll live a hundred years

my thatched cottage
is still fit for writing poems

and I still dream of finding
the lost Peach Blossom spring

my troubles have interfered
with life and its enjoyment

I feel like a cloud or a boat
that drifted aimlessly till now.

2

I came to this part of the world
from a long way away

and then I let six years
slip by before I knew it

but I met an old friend
in the midst of all my wanderings

and I let my poems come
from the nearby woods and springs

I'm too lazy now to care
for the fact of my patched clothing

the holes in my shoes don't stop me
from going on excursions

what's my property's boundary?
there isn't one—no limit!

I lose myself
to the river and the sky.

3

The bamboos that I planted
are a riot of blazing green

and the peach trees that I nurtured
burst out in shining pink

the moon in the stone mirror
shines inside my heart

the wind from the snow-capped mountains
blows across my face

here's the red-stemmed writing brush
presented to me at court

and here's the silver tablet
they gave to an aging man

did you think someone
who's lost most of his teeth

would see his name in the list
of official court appointments?

    4

Even though I was sick
I wore a red seal ribbon

and now I've come back home
to pace the purple moss

here in my thatched cottage
I've plans for my old age

I had no business at headquarters
among the gifted younger men . . .

the sun's rays seem to curl
around the soaring swallows

the leaves of water plants
open for the diving gulls

my neighbors send me fresh-caught fish
and now and then a turtle

and ask me very often
to come and visit them.

(HUNG 262–263.) Hung includes only the third and fourth poems of this sequence. A thoughtful series from 765, stemming from the return to the cottage. The stone mirror mentioned in the third poem is glossed by Hung as a "locality in the neighborhood . . . where a large stone slab was said to be the monument of the grave of a mythological queen."

9. East to Kuizhou, 765–766

Sometime in the spring or summer of 765 Du Fu and his family began a journey east by river that took them to Kuizhou, on the Yangzi, where they would spend three years and he would produce a number of especially fine poems. The journey took some time, as it was interrupted by bouts of illness during which the poet was too sick to travel. They spent the winter of 765 in Yunan, where several poems were written.

Leaning on my son
and on my staff as well

because I have been sick
through autumn into winter

my hair is white and now
I rarely wash it

my winter robe
too big for me, too long

I see you are afraid
that I will die

so both of us are tearful
at this parting

we know as much about our future
as waterweeds do theirs

listen, when you write
write legibly!

(HUNG 265.) Despite illness, the poet manages to end on a light note. Zhang is
departing, but Du Fu is of course traveling himself. Zhang is such a common name
that it is difficult to say which of Du Fu's many old friends this one might be.

Up from my sickbed
back there in Yunan

moving my household
to White Emperor City

the willows grow apace
spring rushes them and then departs

our boat heads downstream
riding on clear currents

farmers are talking about
the coming growing season

birds are singing and soaring
over the brilliant hills

I hear that the great Yu
hewed these rocks with skill

and made a place, we find,
where the land is almost level.

<hr />

(HUNG 268.) Written in the spring of 766. Yu was a legendary ruler who was reputed
to have built Kuizhou, the White Emperor City, by hewing out the steep rock cliffs
above the river.

Most of these Kuizhou women
have gray hair

still single
at forty or fifty

hard to marry off daughters
in these warlike times

they face a life
of bitter sighs and tears

it's an old custom here—
men sit, women stand

men keep the house
women go out and work

most of them gather firewood
bring it home

sell it for a pittance
to make ends meet.

———

Even in old age
they wear their hair in virgin's braids

adorn it with leaves and flowers
fastened with silver hairpins

use up their strength in climbing
bringing great bundles back to market

or they make extra money
with risky work at the salt wells

makeup and ornaments
don't conceal the tear-tracks

thin clothes, barren fields
cold, desolate foothills

these Wu mountain women
are reputed to be ugly

but how come a famous beauty
was born not far from here?

(HUNG 273.) The difficult lives of the region's women obviously stirred the poet's sympathies. Married or unmarried, they were condemned to lives of hard labor. The famous beauty referred to at the close is Wang Zhaojun, a Han dynasty heroine who was a favorite subject of paintings and folk songs.

My little servant bound the chickens
ready to take them to market

of course they didn't like that
they flapped, cackled, struggled

my family doesn't like to see
chickens devour worms and bugs

but they ought to realize
the chickens will be boiled

should human beings take sides
between the bugs and chickens?

I call out to the servant,
"Untie them, let them run free!"

Chickens or bugs, gains and losses—
it's never going to be settled,

I think as I lean on this hilltop house
and gaze at the cold river.

(HUNG 275.) The companion piece to this is a longish poem (HUNG 274) about keeping chickens and building chicken coops. Du Fu felt that the meat was good for rheumatism, and he enjoyed the comic behavior of the fowls. Here he apparently decides to spare a few that were meant to be sold at the market.

In front of Kongming temple
grows an ancient cypress

boughs like bronze
roots like rock

frosty bark, rain-washed
forty-foot circumference

its jet-black top seems to rise
two thousand feet

the minister and prince
are long since gone

their memory is cherished
through this great tree

from the long cloudy gorges
of the Wu

to the moonlit snowy mountains
of the west

———

I remember when I lived
near the Brocade Pavilion

the temple and the shrine
for Kongming and his prince

and the two great cypress trees
that grew there too

the buildings had faded
the doors and windows were gone

but the cypresses still stood
signs of power and influence

towering skyward
resisting mighty winds

that kind of fortitude
sometimes seems god-given

Providence has helped it
grow so tall and straight.

———

Suppose a collapsing hall
needed such a roof-beam

herds of oxen set to haul it
would turn their heads in disbelief

but we don't need to cut it down
to marvel at it

and it's too far from where
such timber might be needed

and how protect its bitter heart
from things like termites?

But let's admit its shade and branches
deserve to harbor phoenixes

ambitious men, retired men
do not resent this tree

from ancient days there's never been much use
for something of such greatness!

(HUNG 276.) Hawkes comments: "K'uei-chou [Kuizhou] had been part of the old kingdom of Shu and contained a temple to the great Shu statesman Chu-ko Liang [Zhuge Liang], who was one of Tu Fu's [Du Fu's] heroes. The ancient tree of the title, supposed to have been planted by Chu-ko Liang's own hand, stood in the precincts of this temple. . . . Under Tu Fu's contemplative gaze the old cypress becomes first a cosmic tree of supernatural size, and then a symbol of afflicted genius . . . and of neglected greatness." In other words, it evolves gradually into yet another self-portrait.

Evening is walking
up the mountain paths

I lie in the high chamber
here at the River Gate

thin clouds
rest against the cliffs

a lone moon
swims among the waves

some cranes fly past
in silence

far off, a pack of wolves
howl as they chase their quarry

I lie awake
worrying about war

I have no strength, I know,
to set this world to rights.

(HUNG 287.) Du Fu was given some living quarters in a building that he variously
called the West Apartment and the River Pavilion. Times he spent there, on duty
for the governor, he was by himself, his family lodged elsewhere. He grew fond of
these quarters and wrote a number of poems there.

Here in this upper chamber
rain has wet the curtains

chill air from the mountains
moves through this river city

the path on the sandy shore
has to be higher now

when the river recedes
we'll see sharp rocks again

chrysanthemum petals
are sadly scattered

but the distant pine forest
shows itself fresher

rain beats down
on the red lacquer balustrade

brooding as usual
I stand by a pillar on the veranda.

(HUNG 278.) Another River Pavilion poem.

1

Dew turns to jade-white ice
that scars and wilts the maple trees

the Wu Mountains and the Wu Gorges
grow bleak in autumn wind

the river rises, waves
reaching toward the sky

as clouds come lower now
dark on the darkling earth

seeing the open chrysanthemums
brings memories and tears

my hope of going home
is a lone boat, tied up

people are busy sewing and patching
their cold weather clothing

while the sun sets, all through Baidi city
laundry mallets whack.

2

The sun goes down, slanting light
across the Kuizhou city wall

I turn to the Big Dipper
face the direction of the capital

listening to the gibbons—
it's really true

they call three times
and make me weep

unlike the folks of legend
I won't be rafting rivers

far from the incense and official portraits
I lie here on my sickbed

hearing the bugle calls
blown from the whitewashed parapets

and look! the moon
that shone on the ivied cliff

now turns its light to the rush flowers
along the riverbank.

  3

This hilly city's thousand houses
shine in the quiet morning light

I sit here every day
watch the blue hills, the river

after two nights out
the fishermen are straggling home

swallows that should have migrated
are still swooping around

Kuang Heng's candid criticism
won him little fame

Liu Xiang's promoting of the classics
 went against his heart

men I was in school with
are mostly big shots now

good clothes, sleek horses,
homes in the capital suburbs.

4

They say Chang'an
is like a chessboard

and what sad games they've played there
for more than a hundred years

the mansions and the palaces
have other owners now

new civil servants and new soldiers
replace the former ones

but the gongs and drums still sound
beyond the mountain passes

wagons and horses heading west
messages marked with feathers

here in cold autumn waters
the fish and dragons sleep

I live in peace, remembering
my home in better times.

5

In Chang'an, the Penglai Palace gates
face the southern mountains

a huge gold statue holds a pan
to collect night's sacred dew

if you look west you think
of Heaven's Queen and the Jade Lake

look east you think of Lao Zi
crossing the pass in a purple mist

pheasant screens used to open
like parting clouds

and we'd behold the emperor
dressed in his dragon robes!

I wake from my hermit's nap
beside this autumn river

remembering the azure palace doors
when I was at court audiences.

6

From the mouth of the Qutang Gorge
to the banks of Meandering River

it's the same autumn season
ten thousand miles of wind and mist

the imperial procession used to come
from the Flower Tower, along the passage

to wait in Hibiscus Park
for bad news from the front

pearl screens and painted columns
and yellow cranes circling the palace

ivory masts and silken tackle
and white gulls rising up

all the songs and dances—
look back at them in pity!

in that ancient land
that has served emperors and kings.

7

Kunming Lake
created in Han times

imagine the flags and banners
of Emperor Wu

statue of the Weaver Girl
silent in the moonlight

and the stone sea-monster whose scales and fins
moved in autumn wind

wild rice floating on the river
dark under low clouds

cold dew on the lotus
its spilled pollen red

beyond the mountain pass
the sky road only birds can travel

rivers and lakes to the world's end
and one old fisherman.

8

Remembering the Kunwu road
that wound along the Yusu River

shadow of Purple Tower Peak
falling in Meipei Lake

the stalks of fragrant rice
mostly stripped by the parrots

in the emerald parasol tree
nests of the aging phoenix

walking and talking with lovely women
picking up kingfisher feathers in spring

like immortals together in a boat
setting out at evening

I used to write about such things
wielding my writing brush

now I stare into the distance
bowing my white head.

(HUNG 281–289.) This masterly sequence is difficult because the poet lets himself
drift in and out of reverie, thinking of the distant past (Han dynasty) and of his own
days in Chang'an, while anchoring the poem in Kuizhou and the Wu Gorges,
where he composed it during the autumn of 766. He compares his own failure as a
Reminder and an education expert with the difficulties of two Confucian paragons,
Kuang Heng and Liu Xiang. Dreaming and waking, musing and mourning, he
recalls the ways in which the capital city has been luxuriant and meaningful over
the years. He remembers special features of the capital, including a statue of the
Weaver Girl that was supposed to collect dew and a stone Leviathan said to wiggle
its scales and fins and roar during storms. An undercurrent of bitterness runs
through his thoughts about Chang'an; he has spent years longing to be there, a pos-
sibility that he now recognizes as more and more unlikely. Old age and illness have
made him feel irrelevant to the contemporary political scene, and his long-standing
desire to serve his emperor is fading.

Brushwood gates and fences, and beyond
thatched houses, scattered stars

the river darkens and grows waves
raindrops pock its surface

a mountain bird leads fledgling chicks
to feed on wild red berries

a local woman lets me pay her
and leaves me some white fish.

(HUNG 291.) This is the first of a group of twelve under that title. Hung translates
two of them.

The parrot seems
quite melancholy

wise enough to remember
all his missing kin

his green feathers
a bit the worse for wear

his purple beak suggests
he maybe knows too much

he waits in vain for the cage
to open and he'll go free

the branch he thinks he'll perch on
is long since gone and rotten

people pet and praise him
but they tease him too

what's the good of being
a bird who's such a rarity?

(HUNG 293.) Another sly self-portrait.

The year is ending . . . yin and yang
bring in the winter days

the falling snow has stopped—
a cold clear night, here at the world's edge

I hear the fifth watch drum and bugles
a sad military sound

river of stars overhead
trembling above the Three Gorges

people weeping for their war dead
in maybe a thousand households

but early-to-work songs rising up as well
from woodcutters and fishermen

Sleeping Dragon, Prancing Horse
you're nothing but dust in brown earth

and like the letters I don't get
my loneliness means nothing.

(HUNG 296.) The fifth watch is about two hours before dawn. The starry river is the
Milky Way. Sleeping Dragon was the nickname of Zhuge Liang, a statesman from
the Three Kingdoms period whom Du Fu admired (cf. poem 131). Prancing Horse
was the nickname for Gong Sunshu, a Han period warlord who declared himself
emperor at White City.

Here in these Wu Mountains
I spend my time, aging and sick

detained among the others
who are sojourning here

running out of medicine
watching the bushes bloom

last night's rain
has soaked the sandy beach

the spring wind blows
against the river's current

if I were in the capital
they'd be giving me two writing brushes

here I am nothing more
than thistledown in the wind.

(HUNG 299.) Spring of 767. Attacks of malaria had been Du Fu's primary health problem over the winter. The two writing brushes were customary annual gifts from the emperor.

10. The Gentleman Farmer, 767–768

During his last year in Kuizhou (767), Du Fu seems to have attained some prosperity, probably through the generosity of a patron. This is reflected in his buying property in two different locations: a house in Nang-west that he had been renting previously, a spacious villa with a flower garden and a large orchard, mainly of orange trees; and another house, part of a rice farm, in East Village. As Hung remarks, "Thus Tu Fu became a gentleman farmer, much more in earnest than he had ever been. We find him directing his slaves, servants, and hired agents; chopping wood, mending fences, plowing the fields, planting, weeding, irrigating, and harvesting." This period would be brief but productive for him, both as a squire and as a poet.

1

Rivers and mountains
in open sunlight

soft winds
among flowers and spice plants

swallows packing their nests
with mud

ducks basking
on warm sand.

2

White birds mirrored
in the blue river

red flowers blazing
on the green slopes

I watch
this rich procession

thinking
it's time I went home.

(HUNG 305–306.) This was presented as one poem in my *Five T'ang Poets*. I have retained the title I gave it there, "Spring." Hung's title is "Two Quatrains." Note that despite his joy in the season and his new status as a landowner, the poet still feels far from home.

Fireflies
from the Enchanted Mountains

come through the screen
and settle on my shirt

here in my study
my *qin* and books grow cold

outside, above the eaves,
they are hard to tell from the stars

they sail above the well
each one reflecting a mate

in the garden they pass chrysanthemums
flares of color against the dark

white-haired and sad
I try to read their code

will I be here next year
to watch them?

(HUNG 309.) In this case I have translated "Wu Mountains" as "Enchanted Mountains," since the strong associations of magic they carried seem especially appropriate to the otherworldliness of the fireflies.

1

Day by day
the autumn fields grow bleaker

and the cold river
ripples the blue sky

I have moored my boat
in a barbarous country

and made my home
in a western village

when the dates are ripe
I let my neighbors pick them

when the sunflowers are choked with weeds
I hoe them out myself

an old man
doesn't need much food

what's left on my plate I scatter in the brook
to feed the fish.

2

When you come to understand
the laws of nature

you see how hard it is
to change them

deep water
pleases fish

thick forest
suits the birds

now that I'm old I accept
my poverty and illness

I know prestige and power
have burdens of their own

the autumn winds blow on me
indoors and out, table and walking stick

and I don't disdain
a meal of mountain ferns.

3

Music and ceremony
to correct my faults

mountains and forests
to addle me with joy

I nod till my silk cap
starts to slide off

the sun that warms my back
brightens my bamboo book

when the fall wind knocks down pinecones
I gather them

when the weather turns cold
I open the hives to collect the honey

a few last flowers
here and there

in my sandals I stop
to inhale their fragrance.

4

In autumn the sand gleams white
on the far shore

the sunset reddens
the mountain ranges

hidden fish
break water

returning birds
battle the winds

the pounding of laundry
echoes from each house

the sound of the woodcutter's axe
is everywhere

I cannot stop the ministry
of Lady Frost

her white blanket tells me how far I am
from the palaces of younger days.

5

I wanted my picture to hang
in the Unicorn Gallery, the hall of fame

now in old age
I waddle with the ducks and snowy herons

in autumn the big rivers
rise suddenly

at night I hear the waters roar
in the deserted gorges

stones pile up
to block the paths

the sail that might have carried me back
turns into a cloud

and my children grow up speaking
a barbarous tongue

as if they were only fit
for careers in the army.

(HUNG 313–315.) A famous sequence; Hung includes only three of the five. The Unicorn Gallery in Chang'an was where portraits of China's greatest heroes and statesmen were hung.

I

North of the steep cliffs
that belong to the White Salt Mountains

east of the ancient city
on a spur of the Red Cuirass

we have this level site
next to the calm river

surrounded by hills
all of the same height

the haze and frost reduce
bright sun on the warm fields

the rice is ready to harvest
you can smell it in the wind

invitations keep me active
like blowing thistledown

I think I'll just sit down awhile
among these cassia plants.

2

In both our places
East Village and Nang-west

we have the luck to live
next to a cool and limpid river

we have thatched cottages
in both locations

now I stay in the East Village
to oversee my rice fields

and make a little profit
here in the noisy market . . .

there's hardly any path
in this secluded forest

visitors come to converse
with a feeble old fellow like me

some get lost on the way
give up, go home.

(HUNG 316–317.) Two of four poems whose covering title Hung translates as
"Moving from My Nang-west House to Stay Temporarily in the Thatched Hut
in East Village."

I heard you were in a monastery
somewhere in the hills

maybe in Hangzhou
maybe in Yuehzhou

all this time apart
all this war and chaos

through this entire autumn
I've thought and thought about you

my body may be among the noisy gibbons
here in Kuizhou woods

but my spirit floats out to a tower
that hovers above the Eastern Sea

next year in spring I'll sail
down this swollen river

east as far as the clouds themselves
in search of you.

(HUNG 319.) Hung translates the title "For More Than Three Years, I Have Had
No News of My Fifth Brother Tu Fêng, Who Was Alone Near the Eastern Coast."

Just look at this bright mirror
that soared into the sky

the big sword in the song
is enough to split my heart

a spinning thistledown
I have whirled far away

I'm as likely to reach Chang'an
as to grasp that cassia in the moon

the great river of heaven
is white as snow overhead

even birds that roost in the woods
are visible in this light

I stare at the rabbit up there
in that enormous disk

and I can almost count
the hairs upon his back!

(HUNG 320.) The full moon of September 12–14 was so impressive that Du Fu
wrote a total of three poems about it, this being the first. The others can be found
in Hung (poems 321, 322).

Let my neighbor to the west
pick the dates from the trees out front

she's a poor woman, no children,
not much food on her table

if she were better off
she wouldn't need to raid my trees

we try not to embarrass her
we look the other way, in pity

I know you've come a long way
and I don't wish to interfere

but putting a fence up, for example,
would be a bit too much

she's told me the taxation
has skinned her to the bone

what war does to people!
oh, this world makes me weep.

(HUNG 323.) One of his kinsmen, Wu Lang, had taken over one of Du Fu's two houses for him, and he wanted to make sure the old lady next door wouldn't be prevented from helping herself to his fruit.

Vast sky, sharp wind,
and the gibbons wailing sadly

the white sand on the island looks fresh
birds are wheeling above it

everywhere the trees
are silently shedding leaves

and the long river, ceaselessly
comes churning and rushing on

how often in autumn I've stood
a sad traveler, far from home

dogged by my lifelong sickness
I slowly climb this terrace

so many sorrows and regrets
have helped to frost my hair

but now, what's even worse
I've had to give up wine!

(HUNG 325.) Hung feels the high terrace is the one in Nang-west, near the river:
"The poem alludes to the recent abandonment of the wine cup. About a week later,
Tu Fu said in a poem about a party that he would watch and enjoy seeing his friends
drink. Perhaps at this time he was following some advice to try temperance for the
sake of health." But see the next poem.

Well, old Du Fu, that's me
I was a guest at the governor's

I drank too much, I sang and danced
flourished a golden lance

remembering my youth
I jumped up on a horse

started riding madly
through the Qutang rocks

above White Emperor City
above the clouded river

rode straight down that hill
a thousand feet or more

passing white city walls
holding the purple bridle

east toward the hills and level ground
under the high cliffs

riverside villages, country villas
rushing into view

I flourished the whip and eased the bit
and reached the reddish high road

———

I may have been white-haired
but I thought I'd surprise my friends

showing I could ride and shoot
just like in my youth

but the horse, racing and foaming,
may have had other ideas

he stumbled, I fell off,
and hurt myself a lot

carried away to excess—
story of my life

lying in bed, ashamed,
old and in pain as well

———

Friends have come to visit now
I have to get up and meet them

leaning on a servant
and supported by a stick

I tell them the whole story
we all dissolve in laughter

they help me to a picnic spot
next to the clear river

more wine, more food
heaped up in a mountain!

we feast and listen to
music of strings and flutes

we point to the setting sun
won't be here much longer

everybody needs
to drain another cup

but don't ride out too fast
to visit me with comfort

I'm still alive, not like
that poet who was killed!

(HUNG 338.) Hung translates the full title as "Drunk, I Fell Off My Horse and Some Friends Came to Visit Me, Bringing Wine." The closing line refers to Xi Kang (223–262), famous for essays about healthy living, who was arrested and executed.

I feel as old as an ancient philosopher
wearing a pheasant feather hat

I feel as useless in this world
as the famous hermit in the deerskin coat

and I wonder now how soon
I'll go blind?

I've been deaf in one ear
for a month . . .

gibbons will cry
and I'll be spared my autumn tears

sparrows will chirp
but won't make me sad in the evening

yellow leaves surprised me
falling from the hillside trees

I called my son and asked
"Did you hear the north wind blow?"

(HUNG 329.)

I

The world's a scene of struggle
among all living creatures

however strange the place and customs
makes no difference, really

competition
will gradually take over

we start to feel the pressure
we push against our limits

if there weren't famous people
who would feel neglected?

if nobody was wealthy
who'd mind being poor?

eternity is
one gigantic corpse

neighborhoods take turns
weeping and grieving

———

My three years spent
here in the Wu Gorge

have come and gone just like
a candle in a storm

I understand I had to stop here
try to regain my health

I take both grace and insult
with cheerful equanimity

I might have rank at court
but my daily rice is plain

I live in this thatched cottage
east of the city walls

wander the cold valleys
to pick some healing herbs

scratching around in the snow
no fruit-hung vines or branches

————

I didn't follow any discipline
I had no master plan

I've liked a peaceful life
quiet has meant the most

a wise man's taut as a bowstring
so they say

a foolish man is crooked
either that or wicked

I don't know if I'm taut or crooked
and won't pursue the matter

perhaps I'm some of both
I'll warm my back here in the sun

and wait to greet them, coming home,
the herders and the woodcutters.

   2

Late into the night
I sit on our south veranda

moonlight spreads itself
across my knees

a gust of wind has flipped
the Milky Way

sun begins to streak
a nearby housetop

creatures start to wake up
now they've had a rest

they'll set out to forage
along with their own kind

same way I'll wake my sons
and send them out to work

we're selfish, after all,
and need to hoard our food

   ——

Very few travelers pass this way
in this cold weather

the year winds down
and time speeds up

the world is mostly
swarms of hungry insects

because we humans have
this passion to succeed

before we had a history
and grew into an empire

humans were quite content
when they had filled their bellies

but they started keeping records
invented government and education

now we're all snared
in that huge net

———

The man who discovered fire, Sui,
criminal or mastermind?

then the historians came, like Tung,
judging good and bad

anyone ought to know
when you light lamps and candles

moths are going to come
in swarms

but if your spirit can soar
beyond the far horizons

it will find stillness, emptiness
in all directions

and to understand that it's all one—
life and death, going and coming

that is the secret
of immortality

(HUNG 333–334.) As Hung notes, in this poem Du Fu seems, among other things, to express disillusion with Confucian beliefs and values, turning to philosophical Daoism as the perspectives of old age afford clarity and resignation. Sui Jen was one of early China's legendary figures, supposed to have discovered fire. Tung was associated with the first efforts at record-keeping.

Bamboos and mosses
have always pleased me greatly

though I'm like duckweed, thistledown
no permanent address

my children have grown up
following my wanderings

some places we have lived
have made us happy

just consider these flowerbeds
in different shades of red

no brocade can match them
once they start to bloom.

———

I have secured a boat
I'm going to leave the Gorges

I stand here in this orchard
remembering my hoeing

the orioles are saying
February's almost over

today my prow, a painted fish hawk,
is going to fly downstream

I'll think back to the plum blossoms
plucked by the snowy fence

or watching willows bend in wind
there by the pavilion.

———

I'm giving you this orchard
to hold in perpetuity

and making up this song
farewell to rural joys

maybe I'll spend my last days
out on the Han and Yangzi

wherever I go I doubt I'll find
such friends as I've made here

even among the woodcutters
and the local fishermen.

———

(HUNG 337.) Hung translates the full title as "About to Depart from the Wu Gorge,
I Present the Six-acre Nang-west Orchard to Nan Ch'ing-Hsuing."

11. Last Days

In the spring of 768 Du Fu and his family set out on the Yangzi, sailing downstream to Jiangling, some 250 miles. Their original plan was to turn north and go up the Han River toward the capital, but a realistic assessment of the poet's health, along with fresh news of yet another Tibetan invasion, soon put an end to this plan. Instead, Du Fu, visiting friends and depending on patrons, went on exploring the south, making his way eventually to Yueyang in Hunan, on the large Dongting Lake. A local insurrection sent the family on the move again, heading south from Tanzhou. Heavy rains impeded progress, and when the revolt was put down, they returned to Tanzhou. From there Du Fu still had hopes, apparently, of returning to Chang'an. But the winter of 770–771 saw him out on the big lake again, traveling north, and he died on the boat en route.

A light wind stirs
the fine beach grass

the tall mast stands
over this lone night boat

the stars hang close
above the level plain

the moon bobs along
in the great river

will poems like this
ever bring me fame?

age and sickness bar me
from holding a high office

drifting, drifting here
what am I really like?

a lone sand gull
somewhere between earth and sky.

(HUNG 338.) The "level plain" suggests that the poet and his family have traveled
beyond the Yangzi Gorges, heading south.

The lake water's clear
the forest wind's pure

don't go—get off your horse
we'll finish up this wine

I've let my white hair grow
like the crest of a wild crane

what do I care for the neighborhood roosters
telling us all about dawn?

(HUNG 339.) Hung translates the full title as "After Drinking in the Library: I Urged Minister Li to Dismount from His Horse, and I Sang These Lines Under the Moon." He remarks: "In Jiangling he left his boat and took a house. He did not seem to care how much longer he might live, and he took up drinking again. He met his friend Zheng Shen, who was at this time living in retirement in the neighborhood of Jiangling. He also met his friend Li Zhifang . . . who after two years of detention by the Tibetans returned to be promoted to the Ministry of Propriety, and who now had been for several months visiting in Jiangling—probably on leave of absence from court. The three friends now met to write poems and to drink in the library of a certain official, Hu. The time was about April 6, 768."

From your first symptoms
to the end

scarcely more
than a year

I need to show
my love for you

I've turned
the boat around

we were friends
boyhood to old age

so what's death doing
coming between us now

and what will my grief
ever accomplish

my tears splash onto
ground already wet

———

A wonderful man of letters
gone to write in another world

the emperor won't find
a better ambassador

historians will record
all your achievements

poets will keep quoting
your best lines

———

Here at the station
few friends show up

cobwebs
on your coffin

your relatives will have to come
from a great distance

to take your soul and your remains
back to the capital

people will pass the graveyard there
with the giant unpruned trees

and mourn the absence
of a great court figure

spring grass we admired together
fades in the autumn wind

where are you now
you prince among men?

———

(HUNG 343.) In the autumn, Du Fu had set out once again by boat from Jiangling,
heading south. But he was recalled by the news of his old friend's death and felt he
should return to express his loss by visiting the coffin and writing two poems, of
which this is one.

I heard about this Dongting Lake
a long time ago

but not till now
have I climbed Yueyang Tower

the lands of Wu and Chu
spread away east and south

heaven and earth, day and night
are drifting on these waters

no word from relatives
no word from friends

old and sick
this boat is all I have

beyond the mountains to the north
the horses of war are running again

I lean against the railing
tears running down my face.

(HUNG 350.) Du Fu is on the eastern shore of the lake, preparing to sail south.

A white horse comes running
from the northeast

two arrows sticking up
from the empty saddle

and the rider
poor devil

who can tell
his story now?

how his commander
was killed

how he kept fighting
wounded, into the night

so many deaths have come
from this fighting

I start to cry
my tears won't stop.

(HUNG 368.) Evidence of the fighting in Tanzhou that had sent the family on the move once again. The commander mentioned in the poem is likely to have been Cui Guan, the strict, highly principled governor of the region. A disgruntled subordinate murdered Cui and launched the rebellion that forced Du Fu to flee.

The rivers of Hunan
are running high

the sky says
late autumn

who wouldn't weep
at the end of his rope

old age can't carry
sorrow's heavy burden

lots of able men
here at headquarters

fine people, you have done
brave deeds

I'm heading north
into the rain and snow

who'd spare a thought, even a tear,
for this traveler in shabby fur?

(HUNG 373.) Hung translates the full title as "Late in the Autumn, I Am Ready to Depart for the Ching-chao Area and I Leave This Farewell Poem to My Relatives and Friends in the Hunan General Headquarters." This seems to be the next-to-last poem Du Fu wrote, and the last short one.

Acknowledgments

This book came about in a gradual way. I have been translating Chinese poetry for many years now. Sometimes I have worked with others—William McNaughton, Jiann I. Lin—learning much from their expertise with the language. More often, though, I have worked on my own. The Tang dynasty has been my particular focus, and I have come to love the work of many of its poets. Du Fu is one of the five poets who make up my personal anthology of favorites, *Five T'ang Poets* (first published as *Four T'ang Poets: Wang Wei, Li Po, Tu Fu, and Li Ho*, in 1980; Li Shangyin was added in 1990). Subsequently, working with Jiann I. Lin, I translated Yu Xuanji, a woman poet of the late Tang (*The Clouds Float North*, 1998), and then Du Mu, also a poet of the ninth century (*Out on the Autumn River*, 2007).

A friend whose opinion I respect said to me years ago: "Of all your Chinese translations, the ones I like most are those of Du Fu. There seems to be a strong connection there. Why don't you do a whole book of his poems?" I answered then that the prospect was too intimidating to contemplate; but the seed had been planted and, after a considerable interval, it began to grow. Gingerly at first, and then with increasing fascination, I began to trace out the poet's life history, and as I did I also began to add to my existing versions of his poems. Following him chronologically, I realized, would confirm my sense that his poetic development coincided dramatically with the political and historical events that continually impinged on his life, but it would also show me a complexity of relationship between the artist and his art that I could not otherwise have discovered.

As indicated in the introduction, I owe a great deal to the pioneering work of William Hung, who is responsible for the most comprehensive presentation of Du Fu in English. Imprisoned by the Japanese in 1942, he resolved, if he survived, to study Tu Fu (as he spelled the name) with greater concentration. He certainly made good on that by producing *Tu Fu: China's Greatest Poet*, in 1952. Hung's book contains 374 prose translations of Du Fu's poems, chronologically arranged and accompanied by commentary about their circumstances and meanings. The service Hung did the poet, and his would-be readers in English, remains unmatched. I could not attempt to equal it, wanting above all to bring the poems into English *as poems*, but I would not have been able to translate and arrange without Hung's aid, and I have paid tribute to him by correlating each poem with its corresponding number in his book (adding just a few poems that he leaves out).

I should also mention the work of two of Hung's predecessors. Florence Ayscough, in two volumes published in 1929 and 1934, left us versions of 470 Du Fu poems, presented as an "autobiography." Her versions feel dated, but her efforts remain heroic. And Erwin von Zach, between 1932 and 1938, brought out a complete German translation of Du Fu, in two volumes that I have often had reason to consult. Checking von Zach's German versions against my English and Du Fu's Chinese, a conversation among three languages, has often led me to greater understanding.

My debt to Hung is greatest, but Du Fu's other translators have kept me company as I worked, providing information and inspiration of many kinds. David Hawkes's *A Little Primer of Tu Fu* is a kind of translator's dream, with characters followed by phonetic, literal, and prose versions of thirty-five poems, surrounded by helpful commentary. Hawkes is an expert I have consulted many times. I think I first read Du Fu in versions by Kenneth Rexroth, and they remain vigorous and inspiring to this day. Over the years I have come to admire the versions of Rewi Alley, the New Zealander who helped organize China's modern educational system under Mao. And of course I have admired the work of more recent translators such as A. C. Graham, Caroline Kizer, David Hinton, Burton Watson, J. P. Seaton, Sam Hamill, Arthur Sze, and Red Pine. Hinton and Watson, in particular, stress chronology in Du Fu in ways that this book both emulates and tries to enrich.

The critical literature on Du Fu in English is substantial as well, and I found useful insights in Stephen Owen's books, in David McCraw's sometimes eccentric *Du Fu's Laments from the South*, and in Eva Shan Chou's *Reconsidering Tu Fu*, as well as A. R. Davis's biographical and critical study in the Twayne series.

The friend who encouraged me to translate more Du Fu is Lenore Mayhew, and I thank her for that instigation. I owe an immense debt of gratitude to Richard Kent, poet, scholar, and former student, who went over my manuscript carefully, helping me to normalize the spellings to modern Pinyin and checking most of my versions against the originals. I have a comparable indebtedness to Martha Collins, who read my manuscript with the greatest care and helped me shape both the introduction and many of the translations. Other friends who love poetry and know much more Chinese than I do, such as Jiann Lin and Jeanne Larsen, have been encouraging as well, and I thank them warmly, along with my wife, Georgia Newman, always an acute reader of my efforts, and my splendid editor at Knopf, Deborah Garrison.

Selected Bibliography

Alley, Rewi. *Tu Fu: Selected Poems.* Beijing: Foreign Language Press, 1962.

Ayscough, Florence. *Tu Fu: The Autobiography of a Chinese Poet.* Boston: Houghton Mifflin, 1929.

———. *Travels of a Chinese Poet: Tu Fu, Guest of Rivers and Lakes.* Boston: Houghton Mifflin, 1934.

Chou, Eva Shan. *Reconsidering Tu Fu: Literary Greatness and Cultural Context.* Cambridge, England: Cambridge University Press, 1995.

Cooper, Arthur. *Li Po and Tu Fu.* Baltimore: Penguin, 1965.

Davis, A. R. *Tu Fu.* New York: Twayne, 1971.

Graham, A. C. *Poems of the Late T'ang.* Baltimore: Penguin, 1965.

Hamill, Sam. *Facing the Snow: Visions of Tu Fu.* Fredonia, N.Y.: White Pine Press, 1988.

Hawkes, David. *A Little Primer of Tu Fu.* Oxford: Oxford University Press, 1967.

Hinton, David. *The Selected Poems of Tu Fu.* New York: New Directions, 1989.

Hung, William. *Tu Fu: China's Greatest Poet.* Cambridge, Mass.: Harvard University Press, 1952.

Kizer, Carolyn. *Carrying Over.* Port Townsend, Wash.: Copper Canyon Press, 1988.

Lattimore, David. *Harmony of the World.* Providence, R.I.: Copper Beech Press, 1980.

McCraw, David R. *Du Fu's Laments from the South.* Honolulu: University of Hawaii Press, 1992.

Owen, Stephen. *The Great Age of Chinese Poetry: The High Tang.* New Haven, Conn.: Yale University Press, 1981.

———. *An Anthology of Chinese Literature: Beginnings to 1911.* New York: W. W. Norton, 1996.

Payne, Robert. *The White Pony: An Anthology of Chinese Poetry from the Earliest Times to the Present Day.* New York: New American Library, 1947.

Pine, Red. *Poems of the Masters: China's Classic Anthology of T'ang and Sung Dynasty Verse.* Port Townsend, Wash.: Copper Canyon Press, 2003.

Rexroth, Kenneth. *One Hundred Poems from the Chinese.* New York: New Directions, 1971.

Seaton, J. P., and James Cryer. *Bright Moon, Perching Bird: Poems by Li Po and Du Fu.* Middletown, Conn.: Wesleyan University Press, 1987.

Watson, Burton. *The Selected Poems of Du Fu.* New York: Columbia University Press, 2002.

Young, David. *Four T'ang Poets.* FIELD Translation Series 4. Oberlin, Ohio: Oberlin College Press, 1980. Reissued and expanded as *Five T'ang Poets,* FIELD Translation Series 15. Oberlin: Oberlin College Press, 1990.

Young, David, with Jiann I. Lin. *The Clouds Float North: The Complete Poems of Yu Xuanji.* Middletown, Conn.: Wesleyan University Press, 1998.

Young, David, with Jiann I. Lin, *Out on the Autumn River: Selected Poems of Du Mu.* Akron, Ohio: Rager Media Press, 2007.

Zach, Erwin von. *Tu Fu's Gedichte.* 2 vols. Harvard-Yenching Institute Studies, VIII. Cambridge, Mass.: Harvard University Press, 1952.

A NOTE ABOUT THE TRANSLATOR

David Young has written ten previous books of poetry, including *Black Lab* (2006), *At the White Window* (2000), and *The Planet on the Desk: Selected and New Poems* (1991). He is a well-known translator of the Chinese poets, and more recently of the poems of Petrarch and Eugenio Montale. A past winner of Guggenheim and NEA fellowships as well as a Pushcart Prize, Young is the Longman Professor Emeritus of English and Creative Writing at Oberlin College and the editor of the Field Poetry Series at Oberlin College Press.

A NOTE ON THE TYPE

This book was set in Janson, a typeface long thought to have been made by the Dutchman Anton Janson, who was a practicing typefounder in Leipzig during the years 1668–1687. However, it has been conclusively demonstrated that these types are actually the work of Nicholas Kis (1650–1702), a Hungarian, who most probably learned his trade from the master Dutch typefounder Dirk Voskens. The type is an excellent example of the influential and sturdy Dutch types that prevailed in England up to the time William Caslon (1692–1766) developed his own incomparable designs from them.

Composed by Stratford Publishing Services,
Brattleboro, Vermont

Printed and bound by R. R. Donnelley,
Harrisonburg, Virginia

Map by Molly O'Halloran

Designed by Soonyoung Kwon